Thieves, Whores & Dinosaurs

Thieves, Whores & Dinosaurs

A Novel By

Jon Davis

FRENCH
PRESS

Published by FRENCH PRESS
281 112th Avenue SE
Suite 5
Bellevue, WA 98004
USA

2012 Paperback, Second Edition

www.AuthorJonDavis.com

Library of Congress Cataloging-In-Publication Data
LC Control No.: 2012937401
Thieves, Whores & Dinosaurs / Jon Davis
2012 Paperback Edition
Bellevue, WA: French Press, 2012
1105
p. cm
ISBN-13: 978-0615650999
ISBN-10: 0615650996

Printed In the United States of America

Also By Jon Davis

EXCRUCIATING BLISS

WHIDBEY

The wind slithered across the long gravel driveway in cold wet darts as I ran to the mailbox. It was a brutal, early autumn I discovered, having run outside to see if a much anticipated royalties check had arrived. Never had I seen such slashing rain. I'd become accustomed to tranquility out on permanently sedate Whidbey Island. These were uncharacteristically violent, unending showers whose mood was tropically indecisive yet glacial in temperature. Having braved such weather, it was disappointing to find just one lonely envelope in my glossy black mailbox. The mailbox glistened at the end of the driveway, dripping wet, and polished lustrously by the rain. Having lived most of my life in the city, it suddenly felt quaint to have a real mailbox instead of some safe-like cubby chamber in the lobby of a sterile condo tower. This was a mailbox with a flag and swinging door, no lock, as they were not needed out here in the safety of pastoral seclusion. How silly and outdated a contraption it seemed, yet so elegant and noble. I'm not sure where the man who designed my house got it, but I wouldn't have been surprised if it had been looted from a museum in East Asia. It was a work of art, as all things should be, and so enchanting I had to pull myself away from looking at it. It's funny, or rather daunting, that we humans are surrounded by gorgeousness, yet become so used to its ornament, its function, and its abundance, we fail to sometimes see the immense charm in something as ordinary as a mailbox someone, somewhere spent a good deal of their life crafting.

The lone envelope I found inside the mailbox was made of heavy paper stock. This was certainly not an advertisement or bill. It was the kind of paper people used to declare an event, like a wedding or a graduation. I just knew the announcement of some extraordinary occasion had to be contained within. I opened the envelope to read:

Dear Marc,

You are hereby obligated to attend a most stately affair aboard my new yacht I've properly named the New Florentine. You might recall me telling you about how the old *Florentine ran aground off Mallorca last fall. It was a truly ghastly scene, like watching a loved one beaten to death by hooligans. But time heals all wounds and so does insurance! I'm sure you'll find my new vessel nothing less than superb. It's more lavish than the last boat, if can you even imagine such a thing!*

Our annual summit is to commence Friday, September 2nd in Seattle at the Bell Harbor Marina at Pier 66, 10:00am PST. No RSVP required as this is an event I am sure you're not to miss. Our trip will conclude Tuesday, September 6th in San Francisco at the Hyde Street Pier.

Your handsome and charming friend,

Halston Levy

PS: If at your discretion you chose to bring a guest or special friend the notion is welcomed (unless it's that dreadful ex-wife or yours. That beast can stay home!)

After I stopped laughing at the letter I folded it and placed it back in the envelope. Walking home, without any care of the trouncing rain, I thought how nice it was to hear from my old friend Halston. Rather, how nice it was to receive a correspondence from anybody.

Inside my home, a modest stone manor on Washington state's sparsely populated Whidbey Island, I found my favorite suitcase, one I recalled buying for a dollar in Hong Kong. Or was it Shanghai? Upstairs in my bedroom I took the case and began packing five black shirts, five black pairs of trousers, two dark coats, black pen-striped socks, underwear and pajamas. Oh yes, and three packs of my favorite Italian cigarettes. After a moment's deliberation I decided to take a fourth pack of cigarettes. These boat trips were often filled with drama. Writers are dramatic people, both by both nature and reputation. I find that cigarettes, not to mention liquor, can somehow coax every bit of excitement there is out of any situation.

Contemplating whether or not to take my usual writing utensils of notebook computer and journal, I decided against it, having reckoned with the fact that I hadn't crafted a full page of cohesive, literary prose in three years. It seemed unlikely that I'd suddenly resume the art of writing just because I'd be surrounded by a bunch of writers.

Along with an umbrella and extra pair of shoes, I set my suitcase in the tiny trunk of my vintage Alfa Romeo. People often assume, rightly, that a man of nearly 40 years of age who drives a convertible as someone who's experiencing a mid-life crisis. I can't think of a better word to describe it. Just a few months ago I found I'd turned in to the most loathed kind of beast. I was the middle-aged artist who wears nothing but black clothes, drinks and smokes without regard for his health, and pursues strange local women for nothing more than sex and scandal. I was the kind of man I'd written about in my novels. Not the kind of man I wanted to be. I needed a change - a drastic one. But being a lonely, brooding creature of too much acclaim and too little discipline, I'd done nothing to counter the path I was so carelessly drifting along. I looked to this upcoming cruise to San Francisco with friends, colleagues, enemies and ex-lovers to shock me back in to the Marc Mulberry everyone knew and either cherished or abhorred.

Four days would pass until I was to leave for Seattle. During that time I would mind my quiet estate, watering by hand the vines of grapes in the greenhouse and picking the small harvest of apples, pears and other fruits, many already dead as a result of the atrocious new season. With the appropriate lawn tractor attachment, I'd sweep up the layers of sodden leaves and other decay shrouding the grounds. Inside the manor I would clean and polish the aged wood floors and arrange all my belongings in perfect order, just the way I found them ideal. Nothing seemed more hospitable after a vacation than returning home to faultless order and cleanliness.

Once, in another life, or so it seems, I considered myself a cosmopolitan. More precisely, I was a foolish boy who thought being near great things made him superior to those without such proximity. I craved the cataclysmic chaos of urban inhabitance, heralded the bevy of delights showcased in every storefront and been led down the path of rabid consumption. I would seek everything I didn't already know or felt I hadn't seen enough of. It was an endless, exhaustive journey to experience all there was on Earth. Time no longer mattered to me. Travelling the globe, paying most of my attention to Europe, without having to keep an itinerary and at a pace I set myself, opened every sensation there was to exhume from inside my soul.

My journey around the world came as a result of my debut novel. Titled *80s Babies*, my publisher and I watched with shock as it steadfastly rose on various bestseller lists. Its success was unforeseen, but certainly not unwelcome. With pockets overflowing with royalties, the means and ambitions to uncover the obscurities of the world I thought myself naïve to were swiftly accessible. In a fashion describable only as mimicking the lives of the affluent, aristocratic characters of my own fiction, I began a transformation. A skin of frugal principles was shed to uncover a falsely affable minor celebrity of promising literary aspect.

My hastily written follow-up, *The Beautiful Beast*, would only further anchor the critical and financial prowess I'd obtained with my first novel. In this sudden era of drastic lifestyle accruements, laziness ensued. Effortless profit was earned as *80s Babies* found its way in to the national consciousness, becoming a popular network television mini-series. The television show rekindled the nation's obsession with the style and crises of Reagan-era America, much as the show mad *Mad Men* had done for the early 1960s. Between packed book signings and television appearances I'd jadedly write my third and most drivel of works, *Pike Street*. The creation of a greedy publisher and a fame-obsessed author, the overtly contrived book touched on no issue relevant to the modern reader and was rightly panned by every critic from Los Angeles to Boston.

Knowing *Pike Street* to be a subpar work, I went on a national book tour almost as a diplomatic mission, hoping to convince readers and booksellers I was still a viable author. These appearances, meant to hedge against the bad press and negative sentiment that was the result of the novel, resulted in no less than 10,000 people asking me the same question: "When's your *next* book coming out?" Not only that, the minor press that was generated by my in-store appearances was usually accompanied with reader responses where people took the opportunity to bash not just my work, but me personally, calling my trademark monochrome wardrobe more neurotic than an art school professor's attire and my arrogance matched only by the sum of the population of France. Ouch. After two months of touring every bookstore in America I retracted from the spotlight. The small glimmer of notoriety I'd received ended up burning me because I'd abused it. Considering all the kudos that'd been heaped upon my first two novels, I assumed my third book would be a smash no matter what it was about. I spent so little time working on my third book I'm not sure I even read the final draft. People were expecting me to cook up something exquisite for them to consume but I put shit on a plate and served it up with a smile. Having read (and suffered through) that book since its publication, the fact there wasn't a larger backlash is a minor miracle in itself.

With money from the *80s Babies* mini-series and the film rights to *The Beautiful Beast* sold, I fled America for Europe in an attempt to divert my conscious from the feelings of self-detest. Onboard innumerable Eurail trains headed for any city that sounded entertaining I began to plot my next great novel. I filled many a note card with ideas. These cards were packed with the most random of details, like remnants of a character's persona, snippets of a chaotic scene, or the climax of a hasty battle between two arch foes. I filled a backpack with these ideas until I landed in glorious Florence. Gradually Italy became a shroud to hide beneath. My benevolent publisher, eager to print the next Marc Mulberry classic and aid readers in forgetting the disastrous *Pike Street*, had hounded me everywhere I travelled. Eventually I grew tired of their pleadings and let my agent simply know I was "somewhere in Europe." I instructed the literary agency to leave me alone until I was ready with my next work. I've always found that it's only when people expect nothing from you can you truly dazzle them.

In Florence, sequestered in a loft above a hat factory I'd rented on an impulse, my great assembly of scribbled note cards were laid bare upon an old craftsman's work table. Like a modiste, mending and sewing the seam of a chapeau, I'd lace the note cards together. Coherency was the most difficult aspect of this puzzle, but as I went these shards of ideas became fused together, chunks befitting others, and at last a story was cultivated. It was a symphony of personal self-analysis and reflection, the notes of which had been previously jostled and frazzled but were now quilted together in to a stunning synchronicity. Before me was not a work of fiction, but the happenings and experiences of my own life. The characters were real, the people I knew and loved, all masked by flimsy, lucent alterations so lazily applied I didn't dare send the manuscript produced from the note cards to my opportunist publisher. I still had a lot of work to do before this work would be done.

The Italian existence is easy. It is the simple consumption of daily pleasures: the intake of the sun, the mother of all life, and the pleasure of the fruition of earth, the father of all nourishment. But Florence, no matter how appealing or restitute of one's senses, became deluged just after my arrival, flooded not by seasonal waters from the Arno but hungry tourists eager to pick the city's blossoms.

With swollen manuscript in tow, I boarded the Eurail again, this time seeking another journey of observation and, if I was fortunate, unearthing a little more of my own buried psyche. Through the lakes of the Lombardy I searched for nature's insight, finding none. And because the money of yesterday's bestselling novels had been quickly spent in lavish Italy, my prophetic return to America ensued. The moment I landed in New York City my publisher called, as if cameras and sensors were placed at the airport and programmed to alert them of my return.

Money. Everyone wanted to give it to me. All they wanted in return was that bundle of five-hundred pages I carried with me.

This is the point where most authors would boast of how perturbed he made his speculative publisher, how he gave them a glance at his words, they salivated, became ferocious, and just when they were at their most fierce, fed it to them. But I am no master negotiator. I was too exhausted. I gave up the prize the day they called. From a New York City hotel room I watched, day to day, as my editor and her staff chiseled away at my Italian masterpiece, emancipating it from the angry, fiery bravado that filled its breath, and tamed it with slashing red pen like various gashes and cuts, casting it in to a formulaic read, one now fit for consumption: *A beginning, middle, and end*. Nothing more, certainly no less. So what if the finished product was missing 150 pages. Smaller books are cheaper to print.

Without protest I let them publish their version of my book. I viewed this edition as the simpleton's adaptation. And like all skilled capitalists, they were right. I made another fortune, restored my image as America's next great novelist, and the pressure to pen another great narrative evaporated. The now familiar vicious circle of publicity and adoration began once more. Those in the press who'd previously been my biggest critics would claim I'd made a comeback. They said I was "back," from somewhere, not Italy, but back from the obscurity of the preferentially forgotten.

As they always do, they wanted more. No bookstore reading or signing proceeded without a horde of readers asking me when I would publish again. They begged for my words, my vision and point of view. And the longer I kept them waiting the more it enthralled them to hear me say, "I'm working on *something*," never specific of course because in truth I was not working on anything. No purpose I could summon would give me reason to have any more of my thoughts and proclamations become subject to the filters of publishing. No longer would anyone's input facilitate or inspire my writing. I couldn't care what anyone thought of my thoughts. I'd already surrendered too many.

As those eager faces approached in line at the bookstores, pleading for me to tell them when I'd stroke their imagination once more with another fanciful volume of digressing angst, it felt of morbid satisfaction to be wanted for my ideas. To know I played a role in many amateur intellectual's fantasies pleased me on a level far surpassing the monetary rewards I'd earned in publishing my stories. Inside every brain that'd read one of my books was a little seed of my own, sprouting and enwinding all the other thoughts inside the mind, not unlike a cancer would.

Once publicity for the book wrapped I was left alone to author another installment. The too familiar, repetitive routine of traveling and chasing fleeting ideas would begin again. Now with more money than ever, the world was mine. Through Oceania I wandered aimlessly, seeing lands of great potential and waste. Up through the islands of the South Pacific and in to China, Korea and Taiwan I witnessed irrelevant customs unwanted back in the West. In India I spotted not customs forgotten, but people, so impoverished they seemed beyond anyone's help.

Missing the pace, cleanliness, and organization of America, I returned to explore a country I thought I knew but found I did not. Through book tours I'd been in most all of the big cities, but always in a stupor, never having the time or attention to discover each one individually. Craving culture, I organized my on own tour of America's great museum cities, from San Francisco, Chicago, and the spectacular Washington, D.C.. My previous assumption of all great art belonging distinctly in Europe was destroyed. Just like my travels in Europe, I preferred to travel via train instead of by air, especially on the East Coat. As much as I adored air travel I'd seen far too many clouds in my day. Over eighteen months I examined every gallery I could find, exploring the heartland of a country I'd ignorantly passed off as unimportant, assuming the people of those lands to be narrow-minded and prejudiced. It was at a county fair in Iowa, surrounded by families, livestock and an all-around infectious jubilance, I came to realize it was me who was prejudiced. I'd assumed that anyone who didn't live in a world-class city was not worth knowing. I was so absolutely wrong.

It was on this tour of the United States that I began my search for a new home. I'd become tired with the New York City hotel suite my publisher had me living in, a place I deemed a writer's sweatshop. I wanted out of New York, not because I no longer cared for that city, but because New York City can only fully be appreciated by leaving it – meaning it is at its most glorious when you long for it, when it spellbinds you, and fills you with such a rapture that the mere comparison between it and any other town makes all other cities on Earth appear as slovenly backwaters. But as I paced myself in all these righteously glorious cities I couldn't help but notice something they all shared. Each city, with its gleaming bright façade of lovely shopping centers and patches of green scenery could not conceal the rotted core one finds as it peels away its skin in order to feast on its nourishing substance. Beneath the flesh of a giant city there is no splendor, no meaning, but only a great wheel of industry meant for polishing the chrome which makes the city gleam.

Seclusion would medicate my baffling furor.

On a large chunk of seafront land on Whidbey Island I would create my greatest work of art. Not a book, but a paradise in the form of gardens, twisting paths, and fruited orchards. These fifty acres of untamed, rocky bluffs and pasture would be sculpted by hand in to Beatrix Farrand inspired gardens that hung over a series of interlinking combed beaches. Anger and frustration at everything and nothing drove me in to a life not of consumption but coveted self-sufficiency. Meals I wanted to grow myself. Several solar panels and a pair of windmill generators made sufficient electricity to power the super-efficient house I would build, a stone manor I sketched after visiting the great castle estates of the Loire valley in France. Like a city, my estate was a wonderland of sights, natural and manmade, private and serene. The recurrent longing to travel came no more. Everything I wanted was with me.

The reclusive life is a virtue clichéd by many of America's great writers. Appropriately in my reclusion the media dedicated to authors and their works trumpeted my move from urban society to pastoral solitude, not with acclaim but disdain, promoting it as the eve of my deconstruction and a sneer by me towards the populous I habitually ridiculed in my writings, as if I was Howard Hughes or something.

Anonymous visitors would become common to my new home. Many young writers from around Seattle, sometimes in groups, would curiously collect just outside my long driveway and stare at my chateau and its gardens. Being that I was outside so much, minding the gardens and the greenery, I was made highly aware of their regular presence. It wasn't their company that was disheartening, as I'm sure many are drawn to my mystique, but their reaction when they would see me. Unlike a normal person or my neighbors even, these young fans would quiver and sometimes run away upon making eye contact with me. Their startled, frantic reactions made me question if I was threateningly gruesome to observe.

It wasn't until a writer by the name of Amelia Haughton arrived on my property and introduced herself, did I ponder my own magnetism. An editor-at-large at a New York women's magazine, Amelia had about her the kind of unfettered ambition only a writer who's never been turned down encompasses, not to mention that naivety that so often accompanies youth. Now her fantastic motivation was fixed on me, as her next big story was to chronicle what I was working on.

Gregarious, Amelia Haughton asked me for an interview right there in my front lawn. "If you don't mind," she asserted with contrasting bashfulness. In the library of my home I served Amelia ginger peach tea and agreed to answer any question she asked of me. We talked, not so much in an interviewing fashion but more in a flirtatious one. It was obvious we were attracted to each other. The seclusion the estate afforded insulated us from any restrictions the outside world could warrant and the passion within each of us began to burgeon.

Two hours passed during our informal interview when Amelia demanded she leave, asserting she'd overstayed her welcome. Suddenly aware of the stimulation another person provided, especially a beautiful woman six years younger than myself, I entreated Amelia to stay. She declined and walked out after thanking me for what she called an "exquisite affair." I watched as she walked the length of my driveway and through the spot in the shrubs from where she had emerged. Moments passed and I thought how odd it was that such a wonderful, haunting woman suddenly appeared to ask me meaningless questions she hadn't even written down the answers to. For a moment I considered the incident to be a possible hallucination.

The figure of the peculiar woman appeared again at the end of my driveway. I could see she was walking back up to the house. Excited, I went to the courtyard to meet her.

"Did you think of another question to ask me?" I implored, trying to be cute.

"No," she replied without amusement. "My car is gone… I think it was stolen."

It seemed to be fate. Her rental car was stolen and she knew no one other than me on the island. I proposed to drive her back to the city and she accepted the offer. On the trip to Sea-Tac we stopped for dinner, an event years later we'd regard as our first date. After dinner we drove back to my house and she stayed for a couple days, in which time we fell in love.

Amelia Haughton became my liaison with the outside world, jetting back and forth between my country house in Washington State and her job in New York City. She would appoint herself my greatest and most devoted publicist, writing numerous stories about my curious seclusion and the alleged library of significant work I'd kept from my publisher.

Amelia's routine absence to attend work in New York would thoroughly reinforce my affections for her. Less than a year after our meeting I would propose marriage, she would accept, and we'd wed two months later at the Island County courthouse with our only witness a paralegal and my labrador, Miller, who always accompanied us on our way in to town.

After our wedding the unbound lust that seemed to drive our romance slowly progressed towards conclusion. Amelia lived out of her Manhattan apartment during the week and would fly out to see me every other weekend. In all, she spent about eight months of the year in New York, taking extra time off in the winter and summer to spend time with me. Other husbands may have felt neglected, jealous of their wife's busy professional existence, but I felt our arrangement to be perfection. I needed my space, not some maternal spouse who fawned over me. Furthermore, Amelia and I were both devout individualists; marriage wouldn't change our convictions.

Amelia Haughton did not understand the pleasure I felt from living in my world of isolated simplicity. She sought urbane bedlam, as did her overly dismissive, patronizingly cliché Manhattan squad of girlfriends. In marrying her I'd failed to identify Amelia as a complacent, die-hard New Yorker who'd complain of having to fly to Seattle every time she wanted to see me. She cherished her diminutive apartment she struggled to afford in New York City, the Big Apple being the one thing she could see no errors in.

To Amelia, everything outside New York was deficient. In places, people, meals and art she saw not what shined but what lacked. At one point in my life I was just like her, but I'd grown out of that phase and came to know so much of the world that I couldn't ever say one city was going to be my permanent home, although Manhattan did hold a special place in my heart. To Amelia, even I, her husband, was up for critique. Many times in a despondent zeal, usually over my unwillingness to leave Whidbey Island for that of Manhattan, Amelia would accuse me of being an escapist, and a recluse scared of what he didn't know and even more terrified of what he did. Her assessment of me was not just inaccurate, but petty. Couples entrust each other with the knowledge of their faults. When someone in a relationship exposes their partner to their own faults, no matter how glaring, the relationship's foundation will inevitably fracture. In contemplating why she'd married me, knowing I was a selfish hermit, my friend Halston Levy, a successful author himself, would grumble at my sightlessness. He saw it laughable that I was unable to see how a fairly inexperienced and only moderately successful periodicals contributor, Amelia, would leap at the chance of marrying me, a thoroughbred in modern literature. How her career must have been instantaneously embossed being Mrs. Mulberry. His was a stunning observation.

I divorced Amelia Haughton-Mulberry in the fourth year of our marriage. She never left blessed New York to ask me why, never demanded reconsideration. We separated amicably without one financial squabble. When I called her to ask if I should send any of her belongings at the house to her she declined.

"Let them be souvenirs, Marc," she'd tell me, ending our marriage why she was interviewing another writer, either for the magazine or for marriage, I'm not certain which. As if we were meant to be friends and not lovers, weeks and months would pass and a sort of sobriety would set in on us both. Eventually we'd chuckle of how foolish our marriage had been. She'd eventually confess to hunting me down – admitting that the day she met me on my front lawn was not simply with the intention of interviewing me. She'd seen my picture on the back of my books, heard of the circles of writers and artists I belonged to and believed all the rumors going around about me, including the ones that claimed I was a sex addict and narcissist. This actually appealed to her. She wanted someone chaotic and fiery, and above all things, rich. I can see now how she was disappointed to find the real Marc Mulberry to be a simpleton, who yes, was passionate about his work, but not to the point he withdrew completely from the rest of the world or infringed ridiculous demands and eccentricities on the lives of those around him.

The last time I spoke with Amelia on the phone I told her I loved her just after saying goodbye. The moment I said it I realized I didn't mean it in the way I used to, or at least thought I did. To my surprise she returned the words. Just as I was about to hang the phone up I could hear her say, "Marc, tell me you'll take care of yourself. You must certainly get lonely out there…" As if I hadn't heard her, I hung up the phone.

SEATTLE

The valet of the Olympic Hotel in Seattle welcomed me by name as I turned my car over to them. The staff at the hotel had come to know me as I'd spent weeks each year there while in the city, doing things like shopping or teaching writing workshops for the Seattle Public Library under the pseudonym of Quayle Dunnfire. The Olympic was a grand hotel, complete in every manner of European elegance and the only hotel I cared to stay at in Seattle. It seemed the other fancy inns about town all had either snooty, pretentious staff or were too modern and hip for their own good. I always stay in a corner suite when at the hotel just for the views. Once, long ago, a full panorama of the city could be seen from the balcony of one's suite. Today, except for a sliver of vista down University Street toward the bay, the hotel is encircled with skyscrapers. This hasn't diminished the hotel in the least. In fact, I'd say it enhances it. No longer does it have to compete with the glistening bay or mountain views. The hotel stands as a monument to beauty on its own, curtained from the natural beauty of the city by a perimeter of dull steel and banal glass monstrosities.

The morning was unusually and temporarily sunlit. I'd checked in early, around ten a.m., and could see the bustling harbor so active and alive. Massive ships, all with homeports somewhere in Japan, Korea, or China, were queuing up in Elliot Bay like cars on the freeway. As they approached Harbor Island they'd blast their ferocious horns, so loud the city, a raucous territory itself, shook with gentle passiveness. I smoked a cigarette on my balcony and witnessed the soaring orange cranes of the harbor quickly unload the thousands of giant metal containers stacked in towers on each of these vessels. The act of deliverance was performed elegantly as hundreds of men and women worked in elaborate choreography to align the giant undertaking. Without error or fancy the containers were all removed and placed on rails. Down the steel tracks the cargo would be distributed in a hasty demeanor to the consumers who yearned for their goods. These gluttonous Americans knew not of self-sufficiency but only unending ingestion. I found it a miraculous logistical feat that so many items could be packed on a ship, hauled thousands of miles across the ocean, unloaded and distributed to a plethora of destinations all while staying on a schedule that predicted their arrival to the minute. How such massive and complex projects were performed baffled me.

Taking the opportunity to luxuriate myself, I took a hot bubble bath and anticipated what the cruise the next day would be like. It crossed my mind to call Halston just to confirm I'd be there. The call would also serve as a way to see who else would be yachting with us. Then I recalled the invitation's insistence to do no such thing.

After my bath I dressed and put on a comfortable pair of shoes, then set out on the city streets. In ritualistic fashion I stopped by the big department stores to have a look at the pricey new wares and to see if there was anything that caught my eye. Nothing did, so I walked to the international newspaper stand at the Pike Place Market to pick up their freshest copy of *Il Messaggero*. The market wasn't as crowded as I expected so I took a seat at a café near the end of the shops by Steinbruek Park to read of Italy's current happenings. For a moment it felt incredulous reading of Rome and Milan as I was surrounded by the cavorting landscape of modern Seattle. There are few cities I travel to where I look at it, am awed, and determined its best days are ahead of it. Seattle is one of those cities.

Exiting the park, I sauntered down Western Avenue, AKA Furniture Row, seizing a nostalgic gander in all the shop windows, recalling the days spent in my twenties marveling at these chic palaces of decor. Today there seemed to be many more shops than a decade ago. Overwhelmed and eventually tired of sofa browsing I took a deviation to the Seattle Art Museum via University Street. After a dalliance around the museum I returned to my hotel room to find a message waiting for me on the telephone. An unexpected, sultry woman's voice crooned, "Hello sweetie, I can't wait to see you tonight. I've been thinking about you nonstop. You're my new obsession. I made reservations downstairs at The Georgian for six o'clock. I know you hate fancy dinners but this *is* an occasion. Love ya."

The message startled me. I doubted at first it was for me, thinking the voicemail system must have gone haywire and delivered some playboy's message to my phone. But that voice, I knew that voice. The message *was* for me. It was surely Ashley's voice.

Thrice wed and as many times divorced, Ashley Mulberry is perhaps the most vivaciously unsatisfied woman the world has borne. A renascent student of poetry, constantly distracted by men, travel and other fine things, Ashley is always one to be intentionally fretted over. Forever in a riotous stupor, drama appears to be attracted to her and all the things she does. Her invariable deluge of commotion made me weary of asking her on the boat trip. In fact, for as long as I can recall, avoiding the presence of my sister has been a repetitive habit of mine. But now in her voice I heard something, a tone of fresh liveliness, something absent from all her qualities since she divorced her last husband, the doctor.

When I sat on my bed in order to remove my shoes I found lodged between the two pillows a wrapped and bow-tied gift, about the same size as a shoebox. "The hotel just keeps getting better," I said as I removed the bow and opened the box to find a card, the front of which was a whimsical painting of a grand yacht named the New Florentine. Inside it read:

Marc,

Knowing pop culture has completely overlooked you in that funny little vineyard of yours, I thought it important you read my new book. Certainly we are to discuss it on the cruise this weekend.

Halston Levy

PS: As you know, THE CRITICS ARE FOOLS!!!

Beneath the card lay *Fag*, Halston's twelfth novel. Inside the cover I read it to be "the story of a man so dangerously and intoxicatingly fascinated by a distant friend, one who knows not of his carnal lust, he can't function." All of Halston's books had to with homosexuals. I'd read every one of his books, paying no mind reading of gays, as any good looking man in modern America has certainly come in contact with his share. It was in this manner I'd met Halston some fifteen years ago, back when we were both unpublished scribes attending writing seminars at the Seattle Public Library – the same seminars I now hosted incognito. Halston approached me after our weekly group meeting one night claiming he really admired a piece I'd written on the friendships of soldiers serving in the Middle East. Needy of any positive attention in regards to my writing, I gingerly agreed to have a drink with him with the purpose of discussing literature.

That night we talked about everything but writing and eventually the question of my sexuality was raised by Halston. I would gently break his heart, admitting I was wholeheartedly hetero. I could sense his disappointment, and in not wanting to displease him too much, thanked him for the drink and asked if he wanted to go out to dinner sometime to truly discuss literature. Our friendship, one of an entirely platonic nature, would flourish just as our writing careers came in to fruition. We would trade publishing tales, swap suggestions on plot twists and character names and foster the kind of professional friendship many writers wish to develop but rarely do, we being a reclusive bunch after all. Halston adored me more and more as our friendship bloomed, and on some level I knew he continued to want me in a romantic way. I never confronted him about what I thought his feelings to be, likely because I reveled in the attention, knowing at least one person in the world worshiped me.

In an effort to be extravagant, I ran a bath, my second for the day, and read the first four chapters of Halston's new book. After the bath I discovered it to be nearly six o'clock, so I dressed in a nice new shirt and trousers and made my way down to The Georgian, the city's most genteel of eateries located adjacent to the hotel's lobby. Inside the flagrantly lavish dining room, decorated with gaudy crystal chandeliers and silk drapes towering higher than cedar trees and sparse with occupants, I was seated across from Ashley Mulberry. As she vulgarly cheered my entrance I found not only Ashley's voice had changed, but her look had too. Her formerly short dye-job blond bob had reverted to a more natural, flowing auburn set of locks. She was as frailly thin as always.

"I see San Francisco has done you well," I said, hugging her. "You're radiant."

"I am?" she said, falsely bashful.

"A stunner!"

We sat and reviewed the menu. Just after the waiter appeared to tell us about the fabulous house wines, Ashley began to tell me of her new housemate.

"He's a philanthropist," she bragged.

"Does he spend his own money or someone else's?" I asked.

"Both. But mostly other people's. He founded his own agency. It's a huge success."

"A philanthropic agency?" I asked, never having heard of such a thing.

"Yes. They have clients, such as corporations or millionaires and billionaires. They're job is to find an artistic or humane cause that will result in the most positive publicity."

"Sounds devious," I cringed. "Humanity for publicity's sake? What next?"

"I know, that's exactly what I thought. Thinking they were asking investors to give money to art museums instead of the homeless because the art museums would get better press. But it's completely noble."

"How so?" I was reluctant to believe there was anything noble in giving money to any charitable organization and expecting anything more than a warm, gooey feeling on the inside of one's soul.

"I don't know!" She finally huffed, "He's sexy and I think I might fall in love with him."

"Well he sounds delightful," I teased.

"He is! And he's upstairs right now," her eyes brightened when she said this, as if she was trying to allude to something she'd be doing later on that night.

"Have him join us," I insisted, gesturing at the empty seat between us with my hand.

"No!" Ashley swayed her head.

"Why not? Can I meet him after dinner?"

"Absolutely not." Ashley rebuffed, "I'm never introducing you to one of my boyfriends again. You always frighten them."

"That word, *boyfriend*. You're a thirty-four year-old woman-"

Ashley's expression turned to outrage. "Must you say that so loud!" Her offense at my factual statement was completely juvenile, yet *so* Ashley.

I took an elongated drink of the newly arrived glass of wine I'd ordered, then asked, "What's his name?"

Ashley hesitated, then smirked having thought of a lie. "Bob. He has no last name." She really was determined to keep the man, along with his identity, away from me.

The elegance of that evening was further heightened as the twelve-piece orchestra in the restaurant's main dining lounge began to play Mozart.

"Elvira Madigan!" Ashley moaned with gentle delight upon hearing the song. "I just love this song."

"The song is not called Elvira Madigan," I corrected her. She scowled and wrinkled her forehead.

"Yes it is! It's the only song of Mozart's that I like," she rebutted.

"I doubt that. It's called Piano Concerto 21. It was used in a film called *Elvira Madigan* but Mozart did not name it that."

"Whatever, I don't care," she dismissed. "It's like falling in love."

"Or lust," I jibed.

"Amelia spent part of the summer with us in San Fran. She's such a delightful woman." My sister was always one to launch barbs whenever I did so myself.

"Yes, I know. That's why I married her."

"We took her out to Tomales Bay. Had the most incredible time. Said it reminded her of Whidbey."

"That's nice," I replied lazily.

"I don't get it," Ashley spurted, "you two are deeply in love still. Amelia thinks the *world* of you. The whole three weeks she spent with us it was nothing but an exploration in to your psyche. Truthfully, I've never seen someone so fascinated with another person. Not even those little, teenage pseudo intellectuals that camp outside your house are as enamored by you as she is."

"Just because we're divorced doesn't mean we must be enemies," I carped. "Or does it? When it comes to post-marital relations you are the foremost authority Ash."

"No. It's very sweet you're still friends... friends who have not seen each other in years."

Ashley's involvement in my marriage (and divorce) was an unforeseen liability. Often I deemed the connection between Amelia and Ashley sturdier than the one Amelia and I shared. I often wondered if Ashley didn't maintain a friendship with Amelia just so she could use it to cultivate some sort of leverage against me. Certainly siblings do that.

Despite occasional unsavory topics in our conversations, dinner with Ashley was marvelous. Afterwards we strolled around the wind-swept city, watching people and pigeons, and seeing all that was new and shimmering.

"For some reason," Ashley rambled, "Bob hates Seattle. He says it's a cardboard cutout of a real city."

"Who's Bob?" I asked.

"My..." she almost said boyfriend, "lover."

"Oh yes," I said, recalling his name. "What does he know about cities?"

"I'm not sure. The only thing he knows about is art. And cigars. He's a child."

"Aren't we all?"

Being alone with my sister in Seattle reminded me of the times we'd spent there as teenagers with our grandma in her high-rise condo. Grandma Mulberry was a wispy cosmopolitan – a very modern lady who, once her husband Adrian passed on, set out to live an exaggeratedly embellished life, one I think she copied from *Auntie Mame*. Not a night went by she didn't attend the opera, ballet, symphony or any variety of societal affairs on Queen Anne Hill or the then blossoming Eastside.

In Pioneer Square beneath the restored pergola, Ashley bantered on of how alive she felt being in love. "It's *so* new. As if I've never experienced love before." She giggled hearing her own droll. I figured it was the bottle of champagne she drank at dinner that prompted these emotions.

"Every love is unique," I said, anxious to skip on to any other topic. Speaking of love made me feel inept. It's one thing I will openly acknowledge I don't know anything about. For as long as I can remember, I've pondered how and why love exists, how it manifests and how it digresses, how it corrupts and enthralls, how it perturbs and alludes. Love is a beast, one I've scurried away from. It terrifies me. I want it but I know, perhaps too cautiously, it can destroy a person if not treated with respect.

Ashley and I babbled on about our past lovers and while I told her of my first sexual experience, I considered what a mistake it was to invite her on the yacht trip. I suppose it was because I didn't want to invite someone like my agent or editor, the only two people I seemed to have regular contact with, other than Amelia, who'd been banned from Halston's boat. While Ashley recounted the details of the first time she participated in a bisexual orgy, I began to reel inside, considering just how isolated and alone I was out on my island estate. I was a goddamn recluse with no friends!

For a proper dessert we took the waterfront streetcar up to the market and ordered raspberry tarts at the Montmartre Cafe, just as we'd done as teens decades before.

"How's the book coming?" I asked Ashley. A lengthy, cumbersome silence buffered the space between my question and her answer. For eight years she'd been attempting to pen a full novel. In poetry the woman was a scholar; in literature a dithering prospect, or so I thought.

"Marc, it's going better than expected." Despite the good news she seemed distraught at my asking. Whenever discomforted by one of my inquisitions she'd address me by name.

"Are you blocked? I know this is your first book and all, but even the most experienced writers get blocked."

"I'm done. In fact it's going to be published." She paused, glanced around the little café as if suspicious of surveillance, then said, "It comes out on Tuesday."

"Congratulations!" I hailed. Ashley's face did not welcome my excitement. There was something wrong.

"I should have told you this many months ago," Ashley began, "but I couldn't. I don't usually procrastinate but I really have this time."

"What are you talking about?" My glee resided.

"The book is not exactly fiction." These words crept out of her mouth.

"What do you mean?"

"I know a muse has the right to know she... or *he* is a muse, but I think it would have ruined it." After she said this she clenched her jaw like someone does right before they get slapped.

"What muse? Have I had too much to drink? I haven't understood a word you've said."

"Marc, the book is about you. Not really... but *really*."

Her discomfort now made sense.

"What an awfully boring book," I said, trying to ease both her and myself with a dismissive quip. "I don't care if you wrote a book about me. I just care if it's any good," I said cheerily with a smile. It was a façade of emotion. Inside I wanted to throw the table we were sitting at across the room.

"You haven't read it yet," Ashley prophesized. "I think you should read it - definitely read it before you decide not to hate me for it."

"Ashley, no matter how libelous the thing is, I am not going to be mad at you. Really." My lie was so convincing that Ashley took from her handbag a copy of her book, not coincidently published by the same house which printed and distributed my own novels. Across the top of the book read Ashley in tiny little letters. Beneath that was MULBERRY in great big boldface type in the same font as the ones trumpeting the covers of my books.

"Looks like we'll be sharing some bookstore shelf space."

"Yes," she said, embarrassed by the publisher's unabashed attempt to pass her book off as one of mine. One really can't blame the money hungry publishers. I'm told that fairly precise marketing studies indicate that sales of every author's book within eighteen inches of mine are twice as likely to have someone pick them up and read the inside cover.

We ended dessert with an obligatory hug and a brief chat about the next day's itinerary and what to expect once onboard Halston's yacht. As we parted I could feel the rage I'd suppressed at the café begin to mount. *How dare she write a book about me!* In an effort to calm myself, as walking always tends to do, I strolled down to the waterfront instead of heading back to the hotel. Along the edge of the magnificent bay I found the marina where I was to meet Halston and the rest of the clan of oddities the next morning. In the light of a streetlamp I read the first chapter of Ashley's book, *The Tools of the Artist*. The story took place in an old mansion somewhere near Martha's Vineyard and was about a writer who'd become so rich and adored he could no longer write great stories as the angst and tribulation which once drove his creative furor had been anesthetized by luxury. It was a fairly good book and nowhere did I feel it incriminated me. In fact the main character, Jake Rothschild, was so unlike me I questioned whether or not my sister knew me at all.

NEW FLORETINE

Friday morning I awoke with virile anticipation hearing the soothing trickling of a downpour on the terrace of my suite. For breakfast I ordered an extra frothy cappuccino from room service, which I ate with a soup spoon while reading the early Sunday preview of the *Times*. Inside the newspaper I found a blathering review of Halston Levy's new book, one I'd failed to see anything original in. "At least someone's getting good reviews," I said to myself. Below his review was a mention of Ashley's book. It wasn't a review, as only the superstar authors seem to get full-scale reviews anymore. Her snippet was in the 'Also New On Bookshelves' section. The piece was a brief explanation of the plot and who the book would appeal to. According to the paper: "literati geeks will enjoy a peek inside the world of one of America's most overrated and over-read authors."

The strong espresso made me fidgety. I didn't want to waste the morning indoors so I showered, dressed, and set out down Fourth Avenue toward my favorite bakery called Fleur-de-lis. When I exited the hotel I had a brief chuckle directed at myself discovering just how early I'd arisen from bed. It was not even seven. The cloudy sky made the city feel solitary and dark. But the rain was light and the jaunt to the bakery short. And witnessing the city, so early and peaceful, quiet and romantic, made me question why I'd abandoned it. So easy it must be to live so close to everything one could want. Beguiled, I thought of how fun it would be to buy a loft in the city, one for frivolous and convenient reasons, maybe in one of those giant condo towers on Second Avenue they keep building.

A bum outside the bakery asked me for some money. When I told him I didn't have any he started yelling at me, insinuating I was Jewish in his choice of slander.

Who needs a condo when they have hotels?

Everything in the bakery looked so good I found myself purchasing much more than I wanted or could eat. In a gesture of amiability, I offered the bum outside the bakery a croissant to eat. He called me an incestuous term and suggested I place the pastry in my anus, so to speak.

Back in my hotel room I ate the croissant and muffin and tried to determine what kind of gift I should get Halston Levy, the host of the cruise. My first notion was to buy him wine but I then remembered I'd brought him six bottles from my own estate. So I went to the hotel florist and bought as many flowers as I could carry back up to the room. I don't know what kind of flowers I bought as I'm an absolute fool when it comes to botany and plants (other than grapes). I just knew they were very handsome, colorful and exotic – all *very* Halston.

Shrill expectancy grasped me when I found it to be almost nine o'clock, just one hour until I was to be at the dock. In my hotel room I packed up all my belongings, which, in a matter of one day, were spewed about as if my suitcase had detonated. Rain poured from every orifice of the city's landscape as the concierge summoned a taxi to take me down to the marina. I felt like a fool dragging along all the greenery I'd purchased. I must have looked as if I were on my way to decorate a Polynesian wedding.

Beyond reasoning as to why, taxis, tourists, and other slow moving vehicles bunged every path down to Alaskan Way and the waterfront. So long it took to travel the distance of less than a full mile, I managed to dry completely in the cab, just to be subjected to another spattering of torrent when I did, at last, arrive at Pier 66.

The downtown marina was a showcase of elite nautical vessels, all of which appeared suitable for prime ministers and pop star divas. Halston Levy's boat, The New Florentine, was among its peers here. An upgrade from his previous yacht, I assumed Halston spent nearly every dollar of his book royalties on this, his only home, to cruise the straits and seas of every fashionable region of every hemisphere. For years I'd become used to receiving hand written letters from every expanse of the globe telling me where Halston had ventured to. And now, as I could see across the marina to witness The New Florentine for myself, the excitement of sea travel, a means of transport I'd never considered luxurious or desirable, became appetizing. The ocean was conquerable, isolating. How freeing it must be to sail across the oceans and see nothing but nothingness around you. To know you are truly alone must be liberating and terrifying. Supposing one does not frighten at such a situation, the solitude must be bliss.

But Halston Levy, the yachtsman, was never alone. For a man as rich as he, able to afford something as outlandish as a massive boat, he had with him at all times both his servants and lovers. There were always plenty of both in his life. There was the ship's pilot and navigator, Halston's butler and maid, the chefs (usually two or three), and of course, at least one, if not three or four, boat boys that kept him salacious company. Halston loved men and was a pitiful cliché among novelists. "He has a new lover in every port," they'd say, "just like a true sailor." Halston would not rebuff such an accusation. In fact he would be amused by the attention. He was a man who loved to be the subject of envious gossip as long as it reinforced the idea of him as a philandering thinker. For his business with these men, most in their twenties (some just a few days past 18), were solely for creative purposes. While the perverted can conclude Halston did many wicked things with these men, I, his closest long-distance confident, was never informed of anything sexual or illicit. To me it appeared Halston was lustful of not bodies but the realm of flagrant youth his subjects embodied. I couldn't blame him. Halston's twenties and thirties were an age of oppression, an obligated marriage followed immediately by children, all of it becoming a life he'd carefully abandon for truth and realization. Now at age 51 and a literary icon among homosexuals, Halston had to question what his life would be if it weren't for his missteps. He saw himself in these liberated men, who to them, the idea of a marriage and children seemed reckless, as his refusal to live truthfully resulted in a broken family and grief. Halston never told his lovers of his wife or his offspring, fearing they would consider him less of a godly artiste and just another mortal fool.

Strolling in the downpour along the marina's docks towards the yacht, my courteous taxi driver wheeled my luggage behind me as I carried the mass of dripping flowers. As we came up to the yacht I was nearly convinced something was wrong as no assistant or strapping porter welcomed me to take my luggage.

"They must be terrified of the rain," I told the cabbie as I escorted him up the gangplank on to the ship. The cabbie set my luggage down and I paid him. Just as he retreated to the shelter of his car one of Halton's three boatmen witnessed me boarding the ship and rushed toward me to take my luggage.

"This way Mr. Mulberry!" the young seaman hailed, signaling for me to enter the ship's inner quarters. "You'll be staying in the first guest suite."

I followed him to one of the New Florentine's eight rooms, all of which resembled the finest hotel suites with high ceilings, lush furnishings and thoughtful gifts customized by Halston himself. In my room I found a collection of my favorite classical albums, a set of crystal Tiffany wine glasses with my monogram of MM, Belgian liqueur chocolates and a bottle of chilled champagne.

"Mr. Levy and the other guests are in the aft lounge. Would you like me to take those? I can put them in water and vases."

I handed the young man all the flowers I'd been lugging and took my coat off as he left the room. With unusual interest I inspected my flawless room. For a moment jealousy enveloped me. Halston Levy, the man whose overtly queer fiction I once privately ridiculed for its predictable, melodramatic repetition, had become a very rich man. The linens on the bed were the finest France could produce and the ship in which I now inhabited was undoubtedly worth tens of millions of dollars. Upon realizing Halston's apparent wealth I recalled a saying one of my college professors used repeatedly after the university awarded its creative writing awards, and most of the students were feeling glum having not been given a prize: "An author does not need awards to be a success, only readers."

Something about the room riled me. It was a place built to extract what lingered in the creative mind. It was rich with furnishings, all of them exquisite and one-of-a-kind. They themselves told a story. And for the first time in an extensive period I had an overwhelming compulsion to write. At the desk I took a piece of the heavy New Florentine stationary and began to scribble the introduction to a book, one which had been echoing in my mind for a series of weeks. I wrote:

As a fetus I can hear my mother's heart beat like a locomotive's engine. It reminds me of the time I took a train from Chicago to Des Moines to witness the Baghdad Symphony play for a party thrown my do-gooder socialites. It was a good show. And even though the musicians in the orchestra knew very little about music education, they knew how to entertain their occupiers. It's boring being inside a womb. I always feel left out. Sure, I'm the center of attention much of the time. I am constantly able to hear people rubbing on my mother's stomach, trying to communicate with me. And no matter how hard I scream I can never muster enough noise to communicate back. Being voiceless really pisses me off. Sometimes I feel like the Pope traveling around in his bulletproof glass car. Except this vehicle isn't bulletproof and sometimes I become afraid, knowing just how vulnerable I am on this ride. Sleeping is my hobby and I am very good at it. I am often able to tell myself "go to sleep" and the next thing I know I am waking up several minutes or hours later (I don't know the exact time as I seem to have misplaced my watch). It's fun in here. It's a great escape from my former life as a Wall Street stock broker. I don't remember exactly what my job required, only that I really liked telling people "I work on Wall Street." That was the only great thing about my job. The rest of it was shit. Much too much stress. That's probably why I went bald.

Aloud I read back to myself what I'd written and was astounded. It was unlike anything I'd written prior, and even better, it was completely dissimilar to anything I'd ever read. The voice of this new character haunted me for it had just suddenly entered the frequency in which I drew my fiction. This voice seemed to have no gender, no identity, other than a soul looking for a vessel, completely aware of the world outside its confines. It was a spirit whose disposition was absolutely and prematurely jaded by previous experience even though it had yet to be born. Within this voice was prejudice and judgment, yet it was just a baby. Or was it?

There was a knock on the door of my suite and I turned to see the same boatman who'd brought me to the room.

"Mr. Levy has requested you."

"Yes. I'll be just a moment," I replied. The young man left and I turned my attention back to the page. But now the voice was gone. I'd lost it. Just then I was reminded of how easily distractions were able to wipe away any story I had inside my head. Distractions were the reason why I'd moved away from the city. Seeking solace and hoping to turn out one masterpiece after another I found a place in the country. Yet my prolific era never occurred. I would find that isolation and tranquility could stifle the creative mind too. It was somewhere between anarchy and serenity that stories were harvested.

ALLIES & ADVERSARIES

"Sir, he's really quite insistent now," the boatman sternly proclaimed as I lay on the velvety bed of my suite. I'd drifted off to somewhere. I do that much too often. I suspect it has something to do with this wonderful allergy medicine I'm on. I remember laying down in order to mentally gestate my tale of the fetus and its over-developed conscious when something paralyzed my thought process.

"Is my sister here yet?" I asked the boatman.

"She is. She has been for some time now. You were the *last* to arrive."

Usually these affairs were an exercise in who could be the most fashionably late. I'd arrived moments after ten, as the invitation requested. The boatman's tone inferred a bit of annoyance, as if I'd held someone up.

I followed the robust boatman down a long corridor. We passed by several of the other bedroom suites where maids unpacked luggage in to armoires. I was shown in to the main lounge where I found the other eight guests of Halston's gathered around a central coffee table. My appearance was greeted with a sudden fanfare from the group. Not because my attendance was cherished but it now meant we could depart from the marina.

"Mulberry!" Halston chimed, his giant smile eliciting his adoration for me. As I approached to shake his hand, an act that turned in to a brief hug, I sighted Halston's drastic renewal. His salt-and-pepper hair of years past had gone completely silver, something which would have aged the man if it hadn't been for his radiant tan, smoother face, bright smile, and a more rigid stature I felt immediately upon hugging him.

"Levy, you're looking fantastic," I hailed. "This new ship is amazing, but look at you! You're a new man."

"All the credit should be given to Naples. There's something about Italy that revives a person."

"I know," I established.

"Marc, please come sit with the others."

Before me was a tableau of unconventional personalities each so resolute and severe it seemed a miraculous event they share just one room on a single ship. There was a poet and a producer, a Pulitzer recipient, a has-been and a few never-was who were permitted to waft about in our presence because they were either wealthy or beautiful, some both, the only two requisites in this, the most shallow of all groups I associated myself. This was Halston's idea of haute society.

Speaking brashly of his love-hate relationship with America and Americans, William Zofield, a man I'd known previously only through friends and his daughter Katrin Zofield, also in attendance, stood in a strident vernacular pose at the end of the majestic room professing something. All I heard was, "It all comes down to the lowest common denominator."

As if arriving late to a university lecture, I snuck in to the circle and took a seat next to Tom Reynolds, the nation's foremost authority on military fiction and history, who smiled at me and mouthed "good morning." Tom was not usually so social, being an introvert not unlike myself. Imagining what could have prompted such friendliness, I recalled hearing of Tom's last novel, *Pentagon Games,* being purchased for a record amount of cash by Paramount in Hollywood. The gin and tonic in his hand likely only stoked his affable demeanor.

"Are we stopping in Port Townsend?" the brittle voice of Olive Snow abruptly asked, cutting William off from describing his blissful discovery of New Orleans. Olive was a radiant, delicate figure. Her hair naturally auburn and skin a flawless alabaster. She was a tall woman, almost as tall as me. I imagined she would sneak in to my bedroom later on that night, we'd have sex, talk about how each other had been over the last year, and then she'd retreat back to her bedroom to her sleeping husband, Bryan Madden. Confessing to such a tradition suddenly makes the act seem almost vile or immoral. That was the thing about Halston's little boat rides. Morality rarely boarded the New Florentine.

"We can stop anywhere anyone wants," Halston asserted.

"My friend, the antiquities hunter from Pasadena, said he found the most amazing pieces in some of the little shops in Port Townsend," Olive explained.

"Oh yes," Bryan mocked, "like the pair of allegedly Belgian bergeres he sold you for five grand that turned out to be from Indonesia." The group chuckled at Bryan's depiction of his wife's collecting follies.

"Julian is not a crook," Olive made sure.

"Of course not!" Bryan pleaded. "The three thousand dollar vase dating back to the early Clinton dynasty is a simple treasure," he continued to tease. The group laughed out of politeness and compulsion, but no one was truly amused by Bryan Madden. He was a cynic, a tyrant, and a jealous husband. What this circle of companions hated most about Bryan was that he was a film producer, and not the nurturing, empowering, and visionary type every writer dreams of selling his soul to. Bryan treated literature as if it were an investment property, having bought and sold dozens and dozens of film rights in the past several years, and like most his type, sold them like stocks on the Hollywood commodities exchange. He was not invited to this annual summit but the guest of an invite, and therefore whose presence, no matter how unwelcome, could not be revoked.

It must be noted that my illustration of Bryan Madden is absolutely corrupt and bias as the first time he and I met was not on a ship but in the office of my agent in New York City. It was Bryan Madden who purchased the film rights to my second novel, *The Beautiful Beast*. He eventually sold it to a producer who sold it to a director who liquidated it to an actress who lost it in a divorce settlement to an actor who used the rights and some money loaned to him from an upstart studio to create his own vehicle in which to star. The film, one that nearly missed finding a reputable distributor, imploded at the box office and won several "worst..." film awards, including Worst Actor, Worst Writing (for the screenplay, which I had no part in writing), Worst Wardrobe, Worst Special Effects, and Worst Film, which it won. All this at the same time my third book, *Pike Street*, was being trashed by every fan, critic, and naysayer I'd ever had. To me, Bryan Madden was the emblem of my career's lowest point.

Excluding the reviled film producer, the assembly of artists was a durable group of friends and allies. Unlike other groups of writers I associated with, this clan did not compete, but rather lauded one another. This was a workshop held on an established and one might say elite scale. The core of five writers - myself, Tom Reynolds, Olive Snow, Halston Levy and Katrin Zofield — were attempting to establish a league within America's literati of preeminence and unity. We may not have been the most famous or wealthiest writers in the world but as a group we were certainly the most influential.

"What are you doing for Christmas?" Olive asked me.

"Marc doesn't celebrate Christmas," Halston interjected.

"I didn't know you were Jewish," Bryan assumed.

"He's not," Ashley quipped, "he's an atheist."

"I'm not an atheist," I defended. "I just don't feel compelled to celebrate a holiday which has absolutely no meaning other than to spur the wheel of a greedy economy."

"I say the same thing every December 26th," Katrin submitted. "But the day after Thanksgiving I always feel compelled to go buy a tree and lug out the decorations. I think I just enjoy the routines and tradition of it all. Nostalgia is a powerful thing."

"We should all just bag the Christmas tradition," Ashley proposed, stalking the chrome cocktail cart.

"How could any of you call yourselves Americans if you were to eliminate Christmas?" William, the sole Briton asked. "That and the Super Bowl, what's left? Cancel the Fourth of July?"

"He's right. There is a certain American pageantry about it," Tom Reynolds supposed. "American's do Christmas the best."

The topic of American examination and cultural dissection was one we'd all written and discussed in tiresome length on previous retreats and one we'd banned from further deliberation in years past. It was almost a cliché for a writer to dismantle and scrutinize the world's only superpower.

Just as Katrin Zofield was to offer her opinion, the entire ship began to move and no one seemed to pay attention to her point that celebrities were replacing politicians as sources of social discourse and acceptance. To the covered deck we cheerfully moved to watch as the city's vertically spiked core slowly moved away and the sounds of the cars and people became muted. As we darted across turbulent lanes trafficked by ships rising higher than sports stadiums and longer than skyscrapers, the New Florentine began to feel much less significant and opulent than it previously had. Its luminary clan of passengers were now all the more irrelevant. Once the treachery of the crowded sea became apparent, the group realigned back inside the main lounge along a wall of Halston's latest paintings to discuss the insipid lack of emerging art in our time.

"We've entered a brand new millennium," Halston was first to assert, "but have nothing artistically to show for it."

"God bless capitalism infused with the university," I responded. "The newest generation is informed that its talents are only worth something if there is a monetary interest in what they do."

"How do you mean?" Ashley asked me, always skeptical of my ideas, no matter how under developed. It confounded Ashley to believe her education could be corrupt in any way. She'd graduated from a famous school. To be told her education was a training course within a capitalist mechanism condemned her own principles. For someone to say her alma mater was not an institution, but a brand, overwhelmed her. But as Ashley considered that it was only a corporation eager for new consumers that would mass produce T-Shirts, coffee mugs, postcards and key chains with its logo and slogan on it, which viewed students as customers, its classrooms as assembly lines and their educations as their product, she came to realize her manufactured intellect was no more unique than an automobile assembled in Detroit.

"No reputable university teaches a course whose application can't be found in business," I furthered.

"That's been the case for so long," Tom Reynolds said. "College, no matter how liberal, is a tool of industry to mass produce able bodies and minds."

"So! That doesn't explain why art is shit right now," affirmed Katrin. "Where is the new Picasso? Where is the new Monet? Haring? Basquiat?"

"The would-be Picasso," William Zofield complained, "is working for a multimedia conglomerate somewhere in a fortified Silicon Valley compound behind a computer on a desk in an office with no windows. He has never touched a canvas with a brush because artists are not capitalists. Artists are obsolete."

The room was occupied no longer by the sound of languid discussion but by the distant whooshing echo of ships passing alongside us in the harbor.

"Artists are obsolete?" Katrin asked her father. She was visibly agitated by his statement.

"All the great ones are dead." With such said, William took his turn at the cocktail cart, fashioning himself a whiskey sour. "Please excuse my early drinking but I remain on London time."

"You're surely not just speaking of painters," Olive said, daring William to elaborate.

"We're in the absence of an era," William responded. "Artists today do not create, they borrow. They attempt to innovate but really only modify enough to be deemed original by those too uneducated or mentally feeble to know anything beyond what they see in front of them."

"The artist and the creator are two very different people," Katrin declared. "Art is the interpretation of a reality or statement. One cannot create a new reality every time they wish to create a novel or a painting."

"You've completely misunderstood me," William scoffed and then raised his volume. "Innovation has conceded defeat to marketing!"

"As long as a consumer believes what they are buying is new they'll purchase it," I tried to help clarify. "It's called repackaging! It's been done since the dawn of the consumer-based economy."

"What does packaging have to do with art?" Halston asked.

"Art is a product," Bryan simplified. "Whether it's right or not, art, like gold or stock, is a currency."

"What you're saying is absurd," Olive decided.

"Explain why Warhols and Pollocks or anything near the Impressionist or Cubist eras sell for millions?" I asked her directly.

"They're great paintings."

"I don't think so," William rebuffed her. "These paintings and other works are acquired at auctions where the only people in attendance are representatives from major museums. They make money off of art. Art is a business. Not only that, some of the greatest works of art from the 19th and 20th centuries isn't hanging in a museum, they're stored deep inside secure, bomb-proof vaults right next to gold bullion and precious gems. Great art is its own economy."

The matter of art as commerce was death nailed when a young man, no older than 25, entered the room and sat next to Halston. His name was Giuseppe Tavolo, a young actor who Halston picked up in Santa Barbara while cruising (so to speak) the American Riviera. Halston's promiscuous activities had always been one of the hottest recurring subjects of gossip aboard these seafaring adventures. Even amongst so-called intellectuals, sexuality was of animated debate. Subsequent to our introduction to Giuseppe came greetings from the group of courtesy and warmth. Everyone, including myself, accepted Giuseppe, not as a fellow artist but as a tool of an artist, his function being to quench Halston's sexual appetite. It is this hunger of passion that can interfere greatly with a writer's work if its level is not put in check. Too much passion can drive a writer in to distraction and laziness. Similarly, a lack of gratification can disturb and frustrate even the most fertile minds.

It would have been easy for one of us to judge Halston for picking up nothing more than a gigolo. But to do so would have set a dangerous precedent. Judging Halston's sexual rituals, however distasteful or commonplace, would have had the effect of shining a light on everyone else's proclivities, and not just of the sexual kind. Any trait or habit would have been up for review. Surely I would have been exonerated for my elusiveness in opening up to people and having abandoned the modern world for a life of agriculture and contemplation. Tom Reynolds would have surely been critiqued for the mass of novels he claims to have authored (on average a new 500-page book published on the first Tuesday after every Thanksgiving). It is a secret to no one in the circle he is the owner of what is called a "novel factory," where he proposes ideas to paid scribes, usually college students and other ghost writers, who construct the story lines and often write many of the chapters for him. He will then revise their work, making sure it fits the Tom Reynolds style and finally submits it to his editors and film agents. His commercial success was unrivaled in the group, made all the more clear by the fact every Tom Reynolds novel had been turned in to either a film or television series. No one onboard the New Florentine knew how to better sell stories than Tom Reynolds. He was both jealously and justifiably shunned, in secret, by the group's true intelligentsia of William Zofield, Olive Snow, and our host, Halston Levy, who only asked him on this holiday knowing I would bring Tom Reynolds as my guest if he did not receive a separate invitation.

Similarly reviled was Katrin Zofield. Once a feminist and advocate of women's, gay's, and other minority's rights in the business world, Katrin eventually discovered how much revenue a hit cable sitcom can generate for an author and suddenly changed genres from activism to aestheticism. Her first work of popular fiction, *WoManhattan*, was a tired but witty look at the modern New York late-twenties female lifestyle, or at least an ideal and beautiful version of it. Her cast of characters - a core of five markedly attractive college grads - were ridiculously empowered, selfish, dimwitted, and somehow, relatively successful. Yet this portrayal of women, who'd supposedly worked so hard to enter the corporate ranks with titles they wore as flagrantly as their designer apparel and accessories, cared not of their industries but only the opposite sex. Their bountiful sexual relations were explicitly described with the same tawdry prose found in adult magazines. Her first book was a huge hit and Katrin Zofield was the pioneer of "chick lit." Despite its panning by critics, its popularity enabled *WoManhattan* to jump from page to the small screen as a cable comedy where its towering ratings and ability for controversy proved there remained an audience for melodramatic urban fantasies. Incidentally, my sister Ashley was dazzled by the presence of Katrin Zofield at the summit. In describing Katrin, Ashley used words like "polarizing" and "intuitive," which was fitting as it was women just like Ashley that Katrin had glamorized. There were foolishly malleable playgirls in cities all over the world who longed to be just like a Katrin Zofield heroine.

Disdain for Katrin's exploitation of a tired archetype was trumped only by Olive Snow, the wife of Bryan Madden, the repugnant film producer. Like Katrin, Olive had been a feminist in college, thirsty for power and influence. Unlike Katrin, Olive did not feel enthralled by challenging men or the status quo, as she herself was too demure to lead a rally or stage a protest. Olive's success came from a visceral alliance with the male species. She wanted to love men, not corrupt them. Olive was known to be unstable, emotionally and professionally. Few publishers chose to work with her a second time. Often disputes would arise when she'd decide to drastically alter her work while it was in its final editing stages. She could be volatile and corruptive, but passively, as she was never one to intentionally ruin an opportunity. People who knew Olive felt sorry for her. Even I've said she was her own worst enemy. Olive Snow was conflicted by her emotions, not knowing how to control them or how to override them. It was in her turbulent existence she found the majority of her material. For that same reason I'd fallen hysterically in love with her.

SIBLING RIVALRIES

Often at book signings, upon seeing the mass of diverse readers who've been attracted to my work, I question what it is that draws these people to my narrative voice. As a responsible capitalist I must identify what it is I am selling. After years of contemplation I eventually identified a rebellious charm to my characters. They are all young, witty, and somewhat skewed and neglected by society. Their constant trait is unacknowledged genius and it is this same exact character who'd show up to every public appearance I'd make.

There is the young mother who never had the opportunity to go to college, live in a big city or explore the vast realm of cultures the world accommodates. She uses my books as a temporary escape from her own banality and a means to infiltrate an existence of sophistication and indulgence. There is the young oversexed urban male accompanied by his enlarged ego who believes it is he who is portrayed in my novels, as well as the folk-lit know-it-all, also known as the failed novelist turned academic, who is not attracted to my work particularly but the excitement surrounding it, as if he is studying me in order to author a lecture on different kinds of writers. And finally there is the beautifully gawky suicidal teenage girl, sometimes accompanied by her boyfriend who is a secret homosexual. She does not realize her own beauty or worth and her male counterpart, the drifter looking for solace in a world too abrasive to nurture gentle beings, both have a fate no one who knows them can foresee. To have touched the lives of so many readers, more varied than I could have ever imagined, has been the most rewarding aspect of being a published author. But the life I have forged, when compared to my colleagues on the ship, is unremarkable.

Often I will pessimistically believe my education has been wasted and this craft I persist at to be an attempt at something great, but nonetheless unrealized. There remains a constant impression within me that I am of a different breed of human than most. To say this breed is superior would be false and elitist as I was not born different but chose to evolve separately. The decision to exist outside the mainstream is one every artist must make. It is a requisite for an artist to be woven from a more delicate and receptive material in order to examine each emotion and impression with greater preponderance. It is because of this enhanced sensitivity that many will use perilous substances in order to dampen their ability to observe agony. A long history of debauchery existed within my circle and it seemed only a matter of time before it spilled out from the bedrooms and in to the common areas of the New Florentine.

It was a near relief to be left alone aboard the yacht as we sailed in to the harbor of Port Townsend and docked. Victorian furniture, no matter how well kept or restored, delighted me none whatsoever. And to hear the outlandish bickering of the group continue for more than a thirty minute interlude threatened to become nauseating.

As I sat at the desk in my bedroom and looked over the pair of pages I'd quickly purged on to paper just after stepping aboard, I was met with the sudden compulsion to tear them in shreds. But I did not. There was something worth keeping in those lines of text, though I needed a second and more objective eye to permit any value in them. The inability to judge a sentence's worth has always escaped me and I've never felt a piece I've written to be any good until it is sold and popularized.

Just as I was savoring my much desired isolation, there was a delicate knock on the bedroom door. I took it for the inquiry of the maid until I heard my sister's voice call out, "Marcky?"

"You haven't called me that in years," I said, turning to face Ashley as she sat down on the bed.

"We never talk."

"You're so busy," I said, "it's not as if I don't call you."

"Can you believe William Zofield is here?" she asked, emblematic of her to change subjects during an inquisition.

"It was a surprise," I admitted. "He's a very important writer. If this yacht sinks the headline will read 'Zofield Dead, Several Others Lost At Sea.' He's major."

"He's an *impotent* writer," Ashley scuttled.

"Impotent? How do you know he's impotent? You didn't sleep with-"

"NO! *Creatively* impotent," she restated.

"I've heard he's extremely superstitious. Evidently he opens a bottle of champagne when he finishes a book... and smokes a cigarette too."

"Please! The man is an alcoholic. He used to open a bottle of champagne after he wrote a sentence. But from what Katrin says he hasn't had a sip of bubbly in twenty years," a comment on his inability to put pen to page.

"That can't be." I speculated, "I'm sure he'll die and a whole trove of manuscripts will be found in a trunk or in his attic."

"Don't count on it. Katrin insists he never writes. Just stumbles around his decrepit house in London. She says he just watches TV. Can you believe it? The man known as England's last great writer is a couch potato."

"I wouldn't believe anything Katrin tells you." I warned, "After all, how much attention can she give him? She's a New York snob. When was the last time she was even in England?"

"Are you defending him?"

"I'm just cautioning you on your assumptions. These are observations, its gossip."

"No, you're defending a man you don't even know. You're bedazzled by his celebrity."

"I am not!" This was an honest denial on my part. I did not ever hold William Zofield up to be anything other than an accomplished writer. When Ashley used the word "celebrity" to describe him it sounded incorrect. That was a term for hunks and starlets who pranced down red carpets. Zofield was more infamous than famous. He defied all terms. The term "institution" would have been more precise.

"You are. We all are. It's not a shame to admit it," she blathered.

"I'm not bedazzled. I've never even read one of his books."

"You haven't?" She stood up and began flipping through the albums Halston's staff had provided me.

"Nope," I said, shaking my head in affirmation.

"That one of his about the gardener who romances the countess... it was required reading in college. You should read it. It's very innocent and nice, like all romances should be."

"I don't read romance," I sighed. "I find that kind of work more absurd than science fiction."

"So you haven't read any of his daughter's work?" she smiled cunningly.

"Katrin's books are not romance, they're neo-feminist porn," I corrected her.

Ashley laughed at my clarification.

"You know, I'm documenting this whole trip," Ashley acknowledged.

"For publication in *Neurotics Weekly*?" I joked. She didn't think it was funny.

"No. For my next book."

"Already on your second novel? You're wasting absolutely no time."

"I'm toying with the title right now. Maybe something along the lines of *Broken Souls*," she said, parting the curtains in front of the desk. The light blinded both of us.

"Sounds like an instruction manual on shoe repair."

"Oh, you're right," she reflected, "then maybe... oh I don't know!"

"What's your take on us? That we're tragic or maybe just misguided?"

"No. The book is about writers in general. This group of yours is only the starting off point. I want to detail how most great writers have suffered great loss and tragedy throughout their lives."

"But that's not true," I argued. Ashley laughed at my judgment. To her the only great ones were those who'd sold their work to Hollywood for fortunes or died prior to middle-age with an empty bottle of liquor in one hand and a pistol in the other.

"How can you say that? Suicide, crime, early death. It's all too common in the history of literary icons."

"You're confusing great writers with notorious writers."

"That may be. But you have to admit there is an irrefutable, yet oblique misery about this gang of yours."

Her claim infuriated me, but I did not allow the emotion to register on my face. Already, not six hours in to our voyage, Ashley had exposed herself as an infidel posing as a confidant to my friends. She'd likely already called her publisher in New York to tell them of her gossipy dish on William Zofield and the rest of the group in order to secure a supplement to her advance.

"How about *The Mulberry Group?*" Ashley queried.

"For a title? This is a Halston Levy affair, I'm just a participant," I informed. More laughter came from my sister, now a chuckle of false empathy and repartee.

"You've got to be joking!" she boiled over, "or either you're a complete fucking idiot!"

"What?" I said, in retrospect rather blindly.

"Marc, you are the orbit in which these people revolve. No one here is untouched by you."

"How so?"

"The way Olive Snow looks at you is sickening. She either wants to fuck you or kill you. And that husband of hers, Bryan, I'm positive he just wants to kill you. Whereas Halston Levy, similar to Olive, has such a drippy and noxious admiration for you, I think it is a shame you're not gay just so his fantasy of you can be fulfilled and you can both move on away from this pathetic annual boat ride."

If I didn't have some captivation of Ashley's perception of the group I would have slapped her, which would have been superb material for her new book. But I sat there, staring out the window and at the docks of Port Townsend able to see my colleagues returning from their shopping trip ashore.

"As for Tom Reynolds and Katrin Zofield," Ashley continued, "I feel the two of them have reached such a plateau of commercial success they worry that their wealth has diminished their literary value. In Tom's case, he never had any."

"I know," I rang, "how many times can a person write a novel about terrorists pilfering nuclear weapons and threatening America?" We both laughed at Tom's expense.

The ruckus and chatter of the returning group could be heard down the yacht's hallway as Ashley quickly scurried off back to her room. In order to abandon the shopping expedition she'd told the clique she was suffering from a sudden migraine and just had to take a nap. This was a trademark fib that enabled her to evade any prickly circumstance. Of course they all excused her, not knowing her intention was to come and conspire with me.

MISERABLE PEOPLE

After a charming lunch atop the ship's circular promenade deck consisting of pineapple grilled salmon, Waldorf salad, and espresso sherbet, we reassembled in the library, the New Florentine's most stunning room, spanning the entire width of the yacht and standing as tall as a three story building. It was a great feat of engineering to have fit such a grand room on to a boat. Tall rows of books flanked by an array of white pilasters and other ornamentation hovered yards above our heads. As if it were a museum gallery, original manuscripts and other nostalgia sat housed in glass cases around the library, such as hand written notes by William S. Burroughs and a restaurant receipt signed by Gore Vidal. The bushels of flowers I'd brought our host were now in vases of fresh spring water in all corners of the room. This was the room which Halston Levy was said to have constructed all his stories, although I didn't see a desk, paper, typewriter or computer anywhere in the vicinity. The room was so vast I couldn't imagine anyone finding it hospitable enough to write in. I had always preferred intimate, somewhat cramped but densely comfortable rooms to write in. As a matter of fact, I wrote my first two novels in a converted closet that hidden beneath the stairwell in my Manhattan apartment. How someone could write in a room that resembled an auditorium bewildered me.

"The novel is dead!" William Zofield declared, drunk. It was an opinion shared by floundering publications like the *New York Times Book Review* and many elder authors unable to pen greatness in the fresh new century. With this consensus of pessimism the blank slate was going to remain barren.

"Fuck that," Olive asserted. Sudden aggressive behavior was part of Olive's temperament. She'd always been one to attack and escape. I was certain if Olive had ever been institutionalized she'd be diagnosed with a minor condition of bipolar disorder.

"Absolutely," I cheered her on. I was eager for a battle of wits. Zofield and Snow were two ends of a spectrum, so I did what I could to pit them against one another. Immediately I felt like a cheering louse at a cock fight.

"There's still life in it," Halston made an attempt at diplomacy.

"Excuse me for I misspoke," William remarked. "To claim the novel is dead to a room full of writers is like making a gun control speech at an NRA convention."

"I don't understand some writer's intention to fictionalize highly profiled characters, most often in unflattering or disfiguring means," I said.

"Like that man who won the Pulitzer for proposing Virginia Woolf was a dyke," Halston muttered. "Just because someone looked like a carpet muncher doesn't mean she was."

Katrin guilelessly voiced, "Or relatives of celebrities who, in order to make a couple bucks, attempt to write their biography when, despite their relation, really don't know the person that well." Silence followed by immediate chuckling trailed Katrin's ironic remark. Much unlike her, she turned red realizing she'd just incriminated my sister Ashley and her so-called novel that details the life of someone a whole lot like myself. She was in fact referring to a book written by a cousin of Truman Capote's that was such a huge piece of bigotry and homophobia that its publisher cancelled its printing after receiving so many negative reviews after its galleys had gone out to critics and the media.

"It's a movement!" I declared, squelching Katrin's mortification.

"A *bowel* movement!" William brusquely added.

"Nothing is ever really appreciated in its time. Only when something is physically separated by time from its era and wholly developed can it be accurately scrutinized," Tom Reynolds wisely said, ending our conversation on the topic.

"Here's an idea kids," Halston proposed, "let's forget what's been done and talk about what *hasn't* been done. And by done I mean published. What's everyone working on?"

With such a lewd suggestion presented, William Zofield spat the core of his martini olive across the room in to a waste bin. It was a talent he'd likely perfected over the years. Undistracted, as if William were a child and his behavior commonplace, the group diverged on to a pair of sofas around the library's fireplace to scrutinize each other's works in progress.

"I'm working on about three novels right now," Tom began, "but focusing primarily on one I think I'm going to call *Phantom Force*. It's about a foreign submarine that the Navy intercepts off the coast of Manhattan. They are able to disable it and tow it to Virginia where they discover the vessel is fully automated and far more advanced than anything the U.S. military has ever built. Of course the Russians are suspected but are ruled out after the President contacts Moscow. China, Brazil, India and every other major government is investigated but dismissed as having any involvement in the sub's construction. Eventually it is determined that a shadow military, one separate from the United State government or any branch of the military built the submarine. The book proposes that a large, rich state like California or Texas would be capable of funding its own secret military in order overthrow the union." As Tom told us of his new project I could not understand why he wrote. For as much as I admired Tom Reynolds for his ability to produce work en masse, I still found his stories to be lifeless, nothing but extras in a film without leads, the scenarios both too simple and too vast for anyone to really believe them, and the hero always the same guy: an All-American middle-aged white guy with a wife and kids who works for the government, hates politics and bureaucracy but loves his country as much as he can love anything. As Tom explained the plot of his new book I could already see the movie trailer in my mind. Where most writers looked to fill their stories with artistry, humanity, and, if they worked hard, wisdom and insight, Tom Reynolds books were format, melodrama, repetition, and cliché. For me writing was always about exploration, finding new people, new voices and foremost an attempt to unearth new ideas. For Tom it seemed, writing was an exercise in reinforcing an antiquated format of modern cowboy single-handedly facing tests of national security and international espionage.

"We already have five A-list actors killing each other for the lead," Bryan rejoiced. He was ignored by the group and even his wife rolled her eyes at the immaterial comment.

"I thought it was a novel?" Giuseppe, the mysterious young man in the assembly's shadows chirped.

"Yes, but all Tom Reynolds novels are made in to movies," Olive explained. "The films are usually in pre-production before Tom has even finished the book." A muffled interlude of restrained laughter followed her comment.

"Or started the book," Tom surprisingly acknowledged with a forced frown.

Giuseppe's sudden attention seemed to become aroused finding Hollywood power players were on the ship. This could be his big break, he likely imagined, the fateful connection an unknown, unemployed actor must exploit to better his career. Giuseppe's happenstance was no mistake. Halston had planned for the beautiful Italian hunk to charm the Hollywood producer with his presence and evident visual compatibility for film. It was no concern to anyone that Giuseppe's more outstanding talents rest in the bedroom and not on a soundstage. For him to even call himself an actor was a gross exaggeration. Giuseppe had never appeared in a film or play. He was only referred to as an actor because that's what he told Halston he wanted to be and because the idea of having an actor onboard furthered the idyllic notion of glamour Halston desired these events to resemble.

"Poems," Olive offered blandly, returning us to our topic. "Since the baby it's been nothing but poetry and I have a friend who is a songwriter. We've been working on some stuff, but nothing significant." Olive and Bryan had in the last two years become parents to Bradley Madden-Snow, a last-ditch effort to salvage their peculiar marriage. Of course the baby only fueled their fiery rage for one another. In fact it was a surprise to see Bryan Madden on this year's voyage as just one year ago Olive had announced, in his absence, they were separated and exploring the notion of divorce. It was at the same time she and I began having sex. Now with Bryan present and the rift between them seemingly mended, I began to consuder she may have initiated our affair solely out of malice towards her husband and not from a genuine tenderness for me.

"Marc?" Halston asked me, "What are you working on?"

"Nothing. I'm blocked." It was all I could say.

"That's what you said last year," Halston objected.

"I'm still blocked."

"Have you consulted a doctor?" he demanded of me. At once the innocuous question of 'what are you working on?' became an examination of my mental health.

"It's nothing serious," I asserted. The group was not worried for me. Rather, faces of suspicion encircled me and I conjured that maybe they'd perceived me as a liar. I added, "Although I'm fascinated by the resurgence of existentialism."

"And you're not afraid you're beating a dead horse?" Tom Reynolds countered, "c'mon, that movement is certainly dead."

"What does Tom Reynolds know about dead horses?" Halston stepped in, which was out of character. He rarely defended anyone, but Tom Reynolds accusing me of beating a dead horse was like the Pope accusing someone of being a narcissist.

"I've given up writing," Katrin muttered in accordance, as if to support my answer. To have someone else in the room who felt similarly about writing at that moment alleviated some of the discomfort I was having in being truthful. In some slight way I also felt a bond with Katrin. She continued, "The passion is gone. I can't find a topic." She was one of many writers who'd become more than wealthy early on in their career and retired from her art, no longer feeding off the hunger for being published and popular. A session of grief emitted from the group, as if Katrin were to have said she'd been diagnosed with breast cancer or could no longer reach orgasm. "I've been keeping busy at the magazine and in the community." The magazine she referred to was *W*, where she served as Deputy Editor; her community of choice being that of the Manhattan Artists Colony, a non-profit organization promoting fledgling painters, writers and the occasional sculptor.

"My next book is called *Show Me Your Tits*," Ashley said. "It examines nudity in film. Such as why it is acceptable to show a woman's breasts or crotch but male nudity is seen only rarely, mostly in European films." Her report was a complete fabrication meant to conceal her real intent to exploit the fragility of every artist on the ship. It worked wondrously.

"Men produce films," Bryan declared flatly. "Sexism remains in Hollywood. I'm not celebrating that fact, it's simply a truth. Few male directors have the urge to show cock in their pictures."

"Dad, are you working on anything you wish to share?" Katrin asked William. To be suddenly included in the group's discussion pleased William. He cheerily began to share with us news of his recent labors.

"Yes. There's actually something I'm very proud of," he began. The group was captivated by this glimmering revelation. To hear someone so fabled and precocious as William to once again be writing satiated the group's curiosity. "In my garden I've grown the most beautiful roses you can imagine. The blossoms are the size of, oh I don't know, a croissant. They're absolutely huge. When I get back to London I should email you all a photograph of these babies. 'Spectacular' doesn't even begin to describe-"

"For fuck's sake!" Halston toyed, "next year I'm inviting a whole new legion of writers. Here we have seven of the world's brightest minds and only three are working. What a goddamn joke!" With that we were led out on to ships foredeck to watch the day end. The sun had ignited the sky over the Olympic mountain range, befitting the surrealism of everything that took place aboard the yacht. Everyone chatted gaily, witnessing the burning scenery as we sailed up Admiralty Inlet and toward the Strait of Juan de Fuca.

"Can we see the famous Mulberry Manor from this vantage?" Katrin teasingly quizzed, her faint British accent thickened and exaggerated. "I hear they make exquisite Riesling!"

"They do! I bought a case at Costco last month," Tom Reynolds said.

"You sell your wine to Costco?" Katrin asked me.

"As does Dom Perignon!" I defended.

"I can't imagine a store like Costco being able to sell such a product," Halston snobbishly asserted.

"Why? Because you have a stereotype of the people who shop at places like Costco and Wal-Mart?" I mired.

"You're a complete liar if you say you've never been in a Wal-Mart. It's the world's largest retailer!" Tom Reynolds inserted.

"I love my Wal-Mart," said Giuseppe. "Where else can you by a shirt for three dollars?"

"They have Wal-Mart in Italy?" Ashley asked, unaware Giuseppe was referring to his California home.

"It's not as if I sell to Costco. They buy from my distributor. I can't control that." I further explained, "why shouldn't everyone enjoy the product of my strenuous labor?"

A chorus of laughter followed my comment. For some presumptive reason the group believed me to have a workforce of migrant grape pickers and winemakers. Later the sight of my winery would only embolden their goading.

"They sell your books at places like Wal-Mart and Costco, don't they?" Olive interrogated Halston. She was always an expert in identifying hypocrisy.

"No dear. Wal-Mart is apparently against my agenda."

"Since when do you have an agenda?" she asked.

"I'm just quoting a letter they sent to my publisher explaining why they refused to place an order for my last book. You know, the one that reached number *seven* on the bestsellers list."

"Your gay agenda?" Katrin supposed.

"No. They weren't that curt." Halston elaborated, "they said my book was not compatible with the literary desires of American families."

"*Literary desires of American families?*" William pondered in sarcasm, "I've never heard of such a thing."

"Isn't that an oxymoron?" I laughed.

"And they go and sell my books!" Katrin noted. The sex and language contained within her pages made anything Halston described between two (or more) men appear downright wholesome. Furthermore, it was secretive suburban housewives looking to fulfill fantasies that purchased her books, a massive target audience for such a retailer.

"That's because you're *pro* procreation," Halston cited. "Straight people fucking anyway which way 'til Sunday with the occasional lesbian interlude is perfectly acceptable. I'm not sure any of the ball-busting corporate vamps you herald in your books would ever reproduce but Wal-Mart is not intelligent enough to be so discerning."

"Wouldn't child birth ruin their waifish figures?" guffawed William. His first joke of the meeting pleased everyone.

"Shotguns for sale but no books about two boys in love. It's a tragedy!" Bryan summed.

"*Great Gatsby!*" Katrin ruptured in exasperation, "That can't be it!" She pointed toward a sprawling shingled hillside manor spanning the width of a pristine lawn.

"It is," Ashley confirmed. I blushed having my residence on display and up for critique. It was the first time I became embarrassed to have built such an estate. The irony that I lived alone surely enticed the group for comment but they remained silent, taking in the vantage of beach, gardens, house and giant green house.

"It's Easthampton on the Puget!" William hyped.

"Marc, I knew you were a popular author, but I had no idea," Katrin flattered.

"It's not the books," Halston clarified, "it's the booze. Marc here is a liquor magnate."

"Grapes grow in the Puget Sound?" Katrin asked. The thought of me having income outside of publishing astonished her.

"The vast majority of our grapes are grown in the Columbia Valley. The eastern half of Washington state has the best soil in the world for growing grapes. We bring them over here, crush them, and turn them in to wine."

"If you don't grow the grapes here, what's that big glass building for?" Katrin pointed.

"A dirty little secret in the wine making industry is the flavoring that is sometimes added to wine. I'm not ashamed to admit that we do add subtle hints of other fruits and spices even to the wine to enhance the flavor. That's what's grown in the glass building."

"I would have assumed aircraft," Tom said laughingly.

"Or a soundstage," Bryan added.

"I say pull this boat over and let's have a look around!" Katrin insisted. "And I happen to have brought a wine cork with me."

"Ha!" I snickered, vetoing such a ridiculous notion. "I'm not sure why I drove all the way to Seattle. You guys could have just picked me up."

Afternoon snacks and espresso were served by the elusive yacht staff and the joyous conversations continued until a sharp, arctic Alaskan wind snapped across the bow and chased all us whale watchers back inside.

REBIRTH

I keep an archive of random thoughts made of up of phrases, titles, character names and curious circumstances in order to draw from whenever a creative quagmire has presented itself. For three years I'd filled several leather-bound journals with such incoherencies, some so cryptic and obscure that time had eroded their relevance to my storytelling. Those journals now sat at home in a trunk, completely useless when I needed them the most.

It was night and everyone had eaten dinner and was preparing for bed or whatever they did in their bedrooms. The New Florentine was valiantly sailing west across the Strait of Juan de Fuca, a notoriously rough passage living up to her reputation. It was estimated that we'd be out in the Pacific Ocean and sailing south down the coast of the Olympic Peninsula by dawn.

In my suite I was attempting to contribute to my new manuscript - all two pages of it. Such a paltry and insufficient work it was, I laughed thinking of what my editor would say if he could see what a struggle it was for me to write. Words and sentences used to come so quickly and effortlessly to me, as if I could tune my mind to a certain frequency, that of the creative voice within, and copy down the story it would tell me on to the page. But now I was overly critical of the few passages I'd thrown together and determined they did not really work. There was a neurosis about me now. No longer was I foremost a writer but a critic of grammar and originality. Once there was rebellion in the language of my prose. Hell, I'd been known to make up new words if I wanted to, words that people would accept and adopt in to their own vocabulary. When had I become so fearful?

A moment later I found crumpled, torn pages in my hands. It was the carnage of my failed story of the fetus's monologue. Impulse and anger had collided and took vengeance on the only thing of creative worth I'd been able to cultivate in recent months. Now the story was dead and the relief of knowing I did not have to finish it flushed my anxieties.

There was a tap on the door of my bedroom. I expected it to be Halston coming in to say goodnight.

"Come in," I allowed. It was not Halston who entered but Olive Snow, dressed in her nightgown and moving lightly and discreetly. I stood and approached her, smiling with the most charm I could evoke. She didn't return any such gesture. She was upset at something and as I put my hands around her to hug and to hold her she backed away. She insisted that I not touch her.

"What's wrong?" I asked. She closed the bedroom door behind her.

"I can't this time," Olive fettered. She sat down on the foot of my bed and I sat down next to her.

"Why not?" I begged.

"It's not right."

"I know. We've always known that. What's changed?"

"Nothing. It's just my conscious."

"Since when do you have a conscious?" I tried to joke with her but she was much too tense. She stood up again, likely wanting to distance herself from the bed, the emblem of our former passion.

"I'm sorry," I said, "you don't have to. That's fine. You're married, I get that. I don't want to pressure you. In fact I feel like an ass for even asking why you don't want to cheat on your husband with me."

"It's not that Marc."

"Then what is it?"

"I think he's going to leave me." Olive sat down on at the desk chair and began to cry. As I tried to approach her she again gestured for me not to touch her. "He treats me like a roommate, not a wife."

"Bryan has always been..." I couldn't think of the precise word to describe him.

"A son of bitch," Olive inserted. "We don't even talk anymore. He gets home from the studio no earlier than ten o'clock at night and goes right to bed. I've started sleeping in the guest room because of his tirades. Do you know he actually accused me of sleeping with an actor working on one of his pictures?"

"He's always been jealous of you," I tried to pacify.

"I'm not sure that's it. I think he just hates me. And he drinks more than anybody I know. When we got married he told me how much he hated his father for being a drunk. How his dad caused him to never pick up a bottle. But guess what! Every night when he gets home it smells like he's been swimming in a pool of gin."

"Have you talked to him about it?"

"Talk? Hah! We don't talk anymore. We sneer at each other like two old senior citizens. It hasn't even been five years since we got married and already it's as though he's consumed my entire life. God damn it, I'm such a cliché."

"You're not a cliché," I consoled, and then lit a cigarette.

"Life is a cliché," Olive stared up at the ceiling and then noticed the smoke coming from my mouth. "You still smoke?"

"Yes."

"I don't know anyone who still smokes."

"You know me." I said, then pointed, "But these aren't made of tobacco."

"Weed?"

"I wish. It's some kind of dried bush leaf with mint and other herbs, I think. Entirely organic."

"They've banned smoking in Los Angeles. The penalty is public execution." She was now distracted enough by her own parched humor that I put out the cigarette and put my arms around her. It had been months since a man had held Olive Snow the way she cherished. I recalled the hours she'd spent in my arms in bed, on the beach, or whenever at all possible. I often considered she liked to be held as much as she liked sex. Well, *almost* as much as she liked sex.

"I'm sorry," she whimpered, and vaulted out of the room, leaving me in a broken embrace. Exasperated, I reclined back on to the floor and breathed deeply. How cantankerous Olive was to just sweep in, excite me, and then vanish. What an insult it had been to be rejected so unexpectedly. From her flirty manners all throughout the day I would have assumed we'd be fucking by now, just like the good old days.

I crawled in to bed and considered how Bryan's wallowing could upset Olive so much. For her it was perfectly alright to cheat on him, to make him a fool in the eyes of so many people. I was not naïve enough to believe myself to be the only man she'd been sleeping with outside her marriage. Bryan's accusation that she'd slept with an actor was most likely founded in some facet of truth and for a moment I empathized with him. Clarity now formed in me and I began to feel as used as he must have felt. I was just one of Olive's dicks, a means to get her off and stir the flamboyant cauldron of lust and mayhem she delighted in. It became my assumption that the only reason she came in to my room was to make sure I still desired her. I could understand why she felt it necessary to inform me that we could no longer see each other. It wasn't as if I was standing in her bedroom pleading for sex.

"What a bitch," I cursed, then rolled over and attempted to sleep.

There was a knock on the door. I did not answer it thinking it was the irrational Olive ready to make a partial apology.

"Marc?" It was the voice of Katrin Zofield. I sat up in bed and turned on the light.

"Come in," I said, my voice already groggy.

"I'm sorry, were you asleep?" She tiptoed in to the room wearing the most flattering pair of panties barely hidden beneath a long tank top so tight I assumed she'd bought it when she was a teenager.

"No. I just put my head down."

"I would have expected you to stay up for hours chatting drunken nonsense with everybody else. I guess I'm just used to years past."

"I know. It's unlike me to go to bed before sunrise. If I wrote one tenth as much as I bullshitted I might actually have an impressive catalog of titles."

"Shut up," Katrin scoffed, "I hate publisher's jargon."

"Sorry."

Katrin Zofield and I had always gotten along quite well. She was the only person on the ship who did not possess an ego as large as the ship itself. She was also the only one to avoid drama, unlike most everyone else who seemed to incite it. Katrin was also the most constructive of the group, having pointed out on numerous occasions that the function of the meetings should serve as a means for us to help each other become better writers, not simply bicker about everything we despised, which most often included one another. Her greatest commentary came two years previous when she lambasted all of us with the query: "When will we stop *talking* about writing the greatest book of our generation and actually write it?" This was a question that would resonate with each of us well after the boat ride concluded.

"What's this?" she asked. It was just like her to notice the crumpled pieces of paper on the desk.

"Nothing." My answer did not keep her from unfolding the papers and reading them. Suddenly my work was exposed yet I failed to feel insecure. No matter how bad the writing could have been Katrin would of course point out all its strengths.

"You wrote this?"

"Yes. Of course," I shrugged.

"It's not at all like you," she said with a twinge of astonishment.

"What's that supposed to mean?" I asked with spite, offended she might be suggesting there to be a lack of quality in the piece.

"It's so free and fluid. Your published books, which I adore, have a very formal rigidity about them. But this is different. That's all I mean."

"Then it's a double-edged compliment?"

"I wouldn't say that." Katrin flattened the papers on the desk, smoothing them out as flawlessly as she could get them and said, "Compared to your other works this is a completely different species. But it's entirely incomplete. I'd like to see more."

With that she pecked a goodnight kiss on my cheek and left the room. The story was now born again. Her acceptance had given it a rebirth. Ironic the story be about the precipitate contemplations of a fetus.

BREAKFAST

The morning was clear and chilly. And despite being fully awake, I decided to stay in bed for a while longer to read and deliberate. Of course breakfast would be served to me where I lay so a bedridden disposition was not only comfortable, but expected.

My first visitor of the morning was not one of the ship's staff but the same woman who'd made my night's slumber a charming feat, Katrin Zofield. After she'd left my room the night before I'd spent the rest of the evening considering things about her, such as why she had writer's block and what she hoped to accomplish by bringing her father on the trip. In my observations of him, William did not act nowhere at ease on our excursion and seemed to have only elevated the futile self-esteems of the other travelers. Any delusions of grandeur we could have maintained about The Great Zofield were shattered now having witnessed his feeble arguments and obvious disdain for modernity. Even I was a bit disappointed by the man, as for one dazzling season of literature there shined no brighter beacon of literary promise than William Zofield, in England anyway. He'd been published in over 20 languages and had he continued to publish he would have surely been nominated for the Nobel and just as likely rejected it publicly, as he did his knighthood, proclaiming to Her Majesty in a letter published in the *Times of London*: "Monarchies are history. You and your family of scoundrels and media whores are nothing but dusty relics. You belong in a museum." In all honesty I cannot recall anyone praising his actual writing but rather the outlandish rebellion it contained.

"Are you going to fly home once when get to San Francisco?" Katrin asked me, pulling open the drapes of the bedroom to reveal a sky of dueling pale blues with clouds of grays and purple.

"I don't know. I've always liked San Francisco. Might stick around and see what's new."

"Nothing is new." Katrin insisted, "I was there about six months ago for an honorarium at Berkeley. Spent five days in town, gratis of course, and I can honestly say not a damn thing has changed. Same graffiti, same tourists, same cable cars."

"You hate the cable cars too!" I teased.

"Hate? No. They've just outlasted their practicality."

"San Francisco is an idyllic city to write in. I've always admired its ability to preserve its unique character. And I've never once inadvertently stumbled in to a blighted neighborhood. What is so terrific about San Francisco is its as if they arrived to where they are and said 'that's it. We're here. We can stop building.' Do you know what I mean?"

"Exactly," Katrin concurred.

"How's everything in New York?" I asked.

"It's great. It's New York!" she chirped falsely. I decided to call her on it.

"Katrin you don't have to play that game with me. I'm a former New Yorker."

"Okay. Maybe not great. But *good*. I just bought my first apartment. Alone. Do you know how hard it is to buy Manhattan real estate alone?" She said, digging through the basket of novelties and luxuries Halston had given me, delicately examining each rare find.

"No. I always rented."

"It's not fun. They want to know everything about you those banks."

"Why stay in Manhattan? You could live anywhere."

She gasped, "*not* live in New York City!"

"What? Is that so unfathomable?"

"It's the *Capital of the World*," she proclaimed, outraged, her mouth agape. This was a common assertion New Yorkers made whenever the veritable significance of their city was questioned.

"Is it really?" I asked.

"You have any doubt?"

"Yes I do. I've always felt that New York City became the Capital of the World in the mid-twentieth century because

London and Paris were dethroned due to their involvement in the Second World War."

"If New York is not the capital of the civilized world, what is?"

"There isn't one."

"If you had to choose," she persisted, "what would it be?"

"The capital of art? Paris! The capital of entertainment? Hollywood! The capital of power? Washington! But what all of those are superseded by is money. And yes, New York is the capital of money. But the capital of all things? If I had to choose it would be New York. But I don't have to, so it isn't."

"Marc, you make no sense."

"Tell me Katrin, do those women you write about… do they actually exist?" It had always been an assumption of mine that the perpetually single, effortlessly successful, rich Manhattan bachelorette was a myth that many women had imitated but never captured in sincerity or rudiments, only mocking the blueprint Katrin had drawn in her novels.

"I write about a lot of women. But I think I know what you're talking about. And yes they exist! Your ex-wife was one of them."

"Does every bastard on this ship want to talk about my ex-wife?" I snarled.

"What else is there to talk about? Your divorce is the only notable event of recent memory."

"That's completely untrue. I bought a dog about nine months ago. A very notable event indeed."

"Glad to hear you're not living completely alone."

"Just me, the dog, the wine. It couldn't be more perfect."

"I think you're sexist. Most authors are. My keen female characters are amusing to you because you fail to perceive the ones who actually exist. You're not the first person to assume they are a parable. But tell me, do the men you write about, or rather the eternally youthful man-boy hybrids which you've celebrated and documented, do they exist?"

"Baby, you're looking at one," I joked, sending Katrin in to a fit of hilarity. Then I corrected, "No, *nothing* does exist. Everything's an interpretation. Characters in literature are all so unreal. Too extraordinary. Too articulate. Even the best of the best, the ones who feel and act so real have been dramatized and idealized."

Katrin accepted my statement and sat down at the desk to examine my writings once more, this time to find newness. I'd written seven more pages of fetal spiel during an outburst of mental ejaculation not three hours previous in the middle of the tepid night.

"Marc!" is all she said, and then began to read the pages. I was about to stand and approach Katrin at the desk but then recalled my previous night's desire to rest in the nude, so I remained swathed under the bed sheets.

"You should write these down. I mean in the computer."

"I wasn't expecting to blossom in to an author on the trip. I left mine at home."

"You can borrow mine."

Katrin buoyantly galloped off to retrieve her computer. I quickly stood and put on my underwear just in time to acknowledge one of the boatmen entering the bedroom with a rolling cart of breakfast.

"Good morning sir," he said to me. I returned a smile and let the young man assemble the breakfast on the suite's dining table near the row of tall windows now shimmering with blond sunlight. Katrin returned with her tiny little computer and set it on the desk for me to use.

"Miss, will you be eating in here?" the steward asked Katrin who glanced at me for permission.

"Of course," I said. The young man laid out two breakfasts and lit a pair of candles. I thought the whole scene too ornate but reminded myself of the affair at hand. Every facet of the trip was supposed to be over the top, even if it was an "informal" Saturday morning breakfast. Chic decadence was as casual as it got.

"That house of yours!" Katrin snickered as we sat down to our table brimming with juices, waffles, omelets, sausages, fruit salad, toast, and a butter sculpture intended to resemble San Francisco's Coit Tower but came off looking like a pathetic little yellow penis.

"What about it?" I asked.

"It's ridiculous," she said plainly.

"I know. It's funny, I never realized how elaborate the house was until I saw it from the boat. It started off as a vacation house in the country."

"So did Versailles. But it's also so marvelous. When you die it could be a museum dedicated to you. A very gaudy tribute."

"If I die within the next twenty years, before it's paid off, the bank will be the one who decides what it's used for."

Breakfast was too tempting to chat over so we gorged ourselves and peered out the window, both silently taking in the splendor of the ragged green coastal scenery.

"What do you think of that Italian boy?" Katrin asked. To be tactful I did not tell her I thought him to be a money-seeking whore using Halston for whatever thrills he could seize.

"He seems nice." I replied. "Why?"

"No reason." Immediately she seemed to regret asking the question.

"Are you sure? You don't have any opinion different than mine?"

"Well…" she hesitated for a fraction of a moment, "I'm just glad somebody's getting some."

"And by *some*, you mean sex?" When I asked this she sat down her fork and glared at me in a way both threatening and wicked.

"Yes. Of course."

"Am I to assume you're not getting *some*?"

She feigned bashfulness and then divulged, "It's been a slow year."

"Tell me about it," I said.

"No. I don't think I will."

Tradition would establish the mornings aboard the ship as a time of concentration, solitude, and work. The group was to share with the others a piece they'd been crafting later that afternoon, be it ready for publication or just an experimental work. Together, Katrin and I labored away, translating my scribblings in to her computer and editing it in to a piece packaged and ready for distribution.

Just prior to lunch the group was assembled in the ship's kitchen, only by chance as we were all curious as to what the chefs were cooking. A discussion began about cities – the loathed, cherished, begrudged, and mystifying – a conversation not dissimilar to one Katrin and I had shared earlier in the day.

"Los Angeles..." William added to our 'worst places to write,' to which the crowd groaned.

"Filth. Hate it. Yuck." Katrin bellowed, upholding her New York citizenry.

"The accidental city," Ashley embellished.

Neither Bryan nor Olive, two Los Angelinos, attempted to defend their city. Surely they'd point out they live in Beverly Hills, *not* Los Angeles. And secretly I did not offer my opinion that the town was much too berated to really be that bad. In fact the sunshine (minus the smog) had always invigorated me when I stayed in town. I recalled writing endlessly while staying with a friend in Malibu. Had I mentioned this surely someone would have remarked that Malibu was not Los Angeles.

"You're just saying that because it's the place a good novel goes to be made in to a mediocre made-for-television miniseries," Olive finally defended.

"No. It just isn't a city. I don't care how large it may be in population or economy, it just seems to be pretending," William concluded.

"What about London?" Bryan asked. This was an assault on all who were creative. London was so much a city to even question it was a yearning for confrontation.

"What do you mean *London*?" I had to ask.

"London, like Rome, is a remnant," Bryan bolstered.

Tom took over, "Like so many European capitals, it does not encompass all things that make a city modern. Nothing avant-garde emerges from London."

"Give an example of a *real* city then," William demanded.

"New York, Chicago, San Francisco," Tom began shooting off until he was interrupted by Ashley who sighed with nostalgia having been reminded of her new hometown and our ultimate destination.

"Dear, you live in San Francisco?" Tom asked Ashley.

"Yes. I have for almost a year now."

"I've always wanted to live there," continued Tom, "just long enough to write a big fat novel and then leave it. Like a lover."

"It's very much like a lover," Ashley lingered.

"Toronto?" inquired Halston.

"Do you want to get slapped?" Tom threatened timidly.

"Boston?" Olive asked.

"Without a doubt!" he recanted.

"Tom, you're making no sense at all," Katrin said. "What exactly is your criteria?"

"My gut."

The group groaned.

"And my gut tells me the glimmering new city of the 21st Century will be…" Despite their disdain for the topic the group eagerly awaited what Tom was about to say. "Chongqing."

"Where the hell is that?" I asked.

"China, of course. Has an urban population greater than either New York or London. But you've never heard of it because you're insulated western elitists."

"How do you know of Chongqing?" I queried.

"My publisher manufactures my books there."

"I don't see what its size has to do with anything," Katrin inserted.

"Nothing of course." Tom extolled, "New York has a population one third of Mexico City. Does that make Mexico City superior? No! As I said before, population has nothing to do with what makes a city great. If that were true we'd all be living in

Tokyo." He received a warm chuckle from the group. "Who's to say Los Angeles is superior to Venice because of its population?"

"Oh Venice! We forgot Venice," Olive recollected. Unanimity abounded on the enticement of Venice, how it was vivid, threatened, perishable, and certainly a real, whole bodied city. But as far as modern, it was anything but.

"You can't leave out Florence," I said.

"You people make no sense!" Bryan laughed. "Rome is not a true city but Venice and Florence are. How is that rational?"

"It's not." Halston explained, "that's who we are. Completely irrational beings living lives so unobtainable we're not sure we're living them. We're trying desperately to be eccentric in a world that has seen, done, and tasted everything. We are artists outside an artistic movement. All we can do is be snobs and make judgments on things that are out of vogue."

The now timorous crowd quickly dispersed about the ship. We'd all been exposed as the frauds we proudly were.

CONGLOMERATES

Journalist and friends have depicted me in their works as being a dandy. The idiom might sound as though it refers to one's sexuality or mannerisms but it is in fact a flattering term, denoting a man who pays close attention to his appearance or one who is of first-rate status. Preferential of the former, I do not feel any vainer than the men of France or Italy, my ancestors. But for some reason in America, the man who carefully minds his guise is deemed a weakling, as are all intellectuals, making me a double-weakling.

A fellow dandy, Bryan Madden, had courted me as I sat alone reading over my latest pages on the boats smaller, more private foredeck. Bryan was one of Hollywood's most prolific producers and rumored to be helming the Tom Reynolds adaptation of *Pentagon Games* as director. He was a man of flawless stature with a face made for appearing in films, rather than just producing them. He kept a tan year-round and still remained young looking at 38. His appearance on the deck caused me to stir in my seat, especially after detecting a look of worry on his statuesque face.

"Bryan," I met him. Any ill feelings I had were entirely clandestine to him.

"Are you working?" he asked me.

"No. Have a seat." I said. He rested in the chair closest to me despite their being eight others to choose from.

"Are you sleeping with my wife?" he asked, as if it were a common question, akin to "milk or sugar?"

"No I'm not Bryan," I said calmly. His tone had been calm and I did not expect for him to lunge for my neck or anything, so I added, "not anymore."

"I thought so," he responded, but queerly added the tiniest smirk, as if he'd just impressed himself by solving a riddle.

"Does it upset you?" I asked.

"No. I don't mind," he exhaled deeply and took one long, cleansing gasp. I couldn't tell if he was hurt, relieved, proud, or complacent.

"Bryan, I'm sorry," I tried to add further apology but he stopped me.

"Marc, it's alright. We have an open marriage. She has her lovers, I have mine."

"I know, but we're-" I almost said friends, "acquaintances. Things could get awkward."

"We won't let them," he cheered. With this statement he completely erased my former vision of him. No longer was he a cliché, power-driven, jealous husband, but a man accepting the behavior of his tempestuous wife and her occasional wretchedness. I did not believe it when Bryan claimed to have other lovers for he had a career too consuming for anyone other than himself. The only end open in his marriage was his wife's.

"This doesn't bother you?" I asked.

"No. Would you believe I came to discuss something completely different?"

"What's that?"

"I'm writing a book," he said, adding a modest inflection of fanfare.

"Good for you. What's it about?"

"Hollywood."

"No!" I exclaimed, humoring him. "How much have you got?"

"Three words... the title. *The Glamour Factory*."

"It's a great title."

"I need help on it though."

"Maybe add a subtitle," I offered, "maybe The Glamour Factory: Hollywood Beneath The Gloss?"

"I don't need help with the title," he refuted, "but with the whole thing. I have no idea how to write a book."

"Then why are you writing one?"

"I just feel I have to. I have so many ideas and funny stories about stars and the packs they run in. How the privileged are greedy and undeserving."

"Have you chronicled your material? Kept a journal?"

"No," he said, registering disappointment in himself.

At this point one of the fawning stewards came out to our deck and offered us drinks. We accepted and were momentarily sipping the most ridiculous margaritas ever blended on the open sea, each decorated with necklaces of fruit we could have worn around our necks like Hawaiin leis.

"Where do I begin?" Bryan redirected.

"Just start writing." I instructed, "that's the most important thing. Many first-time authors think that a guy just sits down and writes a book and then it's published. However, editing your material is the most time consuming process, not the actual writing." Bryan listened intently to me as I explained my own queer process in crafting novels. "Experiment. Find what works best for you," I restated. "There is no one way to create a book just as there is no one method in filming a movie."

"Were you being honest when you said you weren't writing?" Bryan asked. He was as stunned as anyone, even in disbelief, that I might not be working. Many people had assumed that my time away from publishing was being spent working on multiple manuscripts and that I would return to the marketplace with a collection of new novels any day now. To hear I hadn't been working on anything was a disappointment to some, and even to myself.

"Why? You want to make an offer on something?" My comment was crude, but remained true to his type. Bryan and his colleagues were notorious for purchasing film rights to books before they were published, sometimes even written. But I read him wrong, true to my own tendency of suspecting malice in everyone.

"No. I'm just trying to be friendly," Bryan rebuffed, his reaction that of confused discontent. He now must have imagined it rude to ask a writer if he was crafting a new story.

"I'm sorry," I said and went back to reading through my work, figuring he'd want to escape my boorish temperament. But he didn't leave. Instead he lit a cigarette, a Firenze, a brand so rare in America I couldn't imagine the likelihood of us sharing such an endangered addiction.

"You smoke?" I said eagerly.

"Yes. I'm sorry, is it bothering you?"

"Yes," I said, falsely numb. Bryan took this as an offense and stood up to leave just as I took out a Firenze of my own and lit it. He now understood my sarcasm.

"If you're not writing, what is this?" he asked of the papers before me.

"A short story I've been toying with. Nothing major. I just started writing it yesterday."

"Can I read it?"

"No, I'm sorry," I said flatly. It'd been standard, long-lasting protocol of mine never to let any pedestrian read my work prior to my editor's eyeing and critique. That rule however, had already been broken by Katrin who'd lovingly perused the new work.

"Do you hate me?" Bryan asked.

"Yes."

"Why?"

"You know why."

"Because of the book?" He referred to *The Beautiful Beast*, my second novel. Despite numerous social encounters we had never frankly discussed the disaster the book encountered when Hollywood adapted it to film. Surely even a pariah like Bryan had some remorse in maligning my work.

"Yes," I replied.

"I had no choice Marc," he claimed. "I was bankrupt. My lawyers took a look at what I owned, your book being part of a multitude of rights, and they sold it. It wasn't my choice. I could have made it in to a wonderful picture. Something similar to the original story, not that glib celebrity exposé they attempted." For

Bryan to acknowledge the adaptation's downfall diminished my lingering resentment for him.

"At least it's in the right hands now," Bryan added.

"Who's hands?" I asked, not knowing what he referred to.

"What?" he speculated, staring at me as though I were attempting false astonishment.

"Did someone buy the rights from... what's-his-face, that actor?"

"Well yeah!" he declared, rejoicing in whatever the significance was. "The corporation that owns your publisher acquired the rights when they merged with the studio that produced the film that owns the distribution rights. Simply put, your publisher owns the film rights to your book."

"So what does that mean?" I was retracing what he'd said in my mind.

"It means the next time you finish a novel and your current publisher wants to buy it, one of your negotiating terms could be that they turn over of the film rights to *The Beautiful Beast* to you, for free."

"It's so complex," I said, nearly befuddled.

"It couldn't be simpler!" Bryan laughed. "How much did I buy the rights to your book for?"

"Two million."

"Which I'm sure you've put to good use."

"I bought seven-hundred acres of grapes with it."

"So you got a winery out of it. And now, if you act quickly enough before your publisher is gobbled up in to some other conglomerate, or worse, fractioned off in to pieces for other corporations to devour, you can have the rights back. Hell, they'll probably give them to you if you just ask. You're their star author. And they paid next to nothing for it."

"What do you consider *next to nothing?*"

"I believe they paid something around seven-billion for about three-thousand films. Where I come from that's pennies a picture."

Bryan's information was of sudden and tremendous worth to me. His suggestion to contact my publisher and negotiate the terms to which they'd give me the film rights, a more symbolic asset now that Hollywood had ruined the book, became of immediate significance. If completely successfully it would correct the one career flaw I'd ever made. Not that owning the films rights would recall the movie but to be in control once again of the one thing I felt defaced my career was in so many ways healing. It was the closest thing to going back in time and making the correct decision I could do.

"This has been the most bizarre and lovely day I've had in a long time," I confessed to Bryan. He smiled at me with a joyous, almost childish grin. Could it be possible he was toying with me? Not twenty minutes prior I'd acknowledged my affair with his wife and suddenly there we were, slurping a second round of blended margaritas over fancy Italian cigarettes, laughing over the foolishness of our business and becoming unforeseen friends.

GIGOLO

Bryan Madden was right! After a brief call to my agent in New York, one who seemed much too knowledgeable off-hand to know the status of who owned the film rights to all my books, negotiations were launched to retrieve what I should never have sold. And according to my agent, a man older than the written word itself (and who'd claim to have invented it if you got him drunk enough), these types of negotiations were becoming all the more common now that the music, film, television and publishing industries were ruled by only about four distinct corporations operating beneath corporate umbrellas large enough to cover all of Antarctica.

I was joyous. Not only for recouping something I'd regrettably lost but for making an ally from a former, if only perceived, enemy. Bryan had retreated to his bedroom to talk to Olive, about what I could only speculate, and I was in my bedroom discussing my next career move with Tom Reynolds.

"If you fucked *my* wife I'd kill you," Tom warned. "She and I might not always get along and there are days I wished she'd die and burn in hell, but I'd still kill you... out of principal." I'd just finished telling him of Bryan's bizarre, almost satisfied knowledge of the spoiled romance I'd shared with Olive.

"I don't fuck old ladies," I joshed. Tom's wife was a full twenty years my senior.

"Me neither," he replied. I didn't know if this was a hint that he and his wife shared a sexless marriage.

Tom Reynolds obtained what no other author on the ship did: gross, undeniable commercial success. He was personally responsible for the deforestation of many woodlands used to make the paper his millions of stout novels were printed on. For all he excelled at in sales he lacked in artistic relevance. Of his 26 published works none had ever been noted for exceptional dexterity or brilliance. An astute reader would understand Reynolds's books to be pages for the masses, the minions, the commoners. He was prevalent, the rest of us were literary and progressive, or at least that's what we told ourselves. This division of writing classes drove a rift between him and Olive, Halston, and probably even William (the snoots) who looked at Tom as an imitator to the craft of writing. I did not know if jealousy of his immense financial accomplishments prompted them to snub him at every opportunity or if they just did not care for him as a person. Potentially both.

"I can never recall why it is I agree to these outings," Tom blasted. We'd opened a bottle of cognac for lunch and were both experiencing the liberating effects it promoted in the psyche. "You're all a bunch of horses asses and sons of bitches!" Tom was mostly serious in his comment but appeared to lack commitment to it once he started giggling at his own statement.

"You come to make friends Tom," I said. When I spoke my face came alive with what felt like jelly spiders tap dancing to the beat of my heart. It was just the cognac but it felt like a peculiar kind of heaven.

"Friends?" he responded in doubt. "I have friends in Chicago, not here. None of whom are as pompous as the likes of you guys. You're all so full of yourselves. So superior! I wouldn't be surprised if you weren't all French."

"I am French. And so are you!" I reminded him

"You know what I mean," he demanded, but I did not. I decided a few more drinks would clarify things.

Olive entered the bedroom in silence, holding an old-fashioned camera, the ones that used real film. She began clicking away at the scene which bothered Tom who'd closed his eyes and was resting his head on the back of the sofa.

"No pictures. I haven't done my hair!" Tom bellowed. This was apparently hilarious to him and he rolled off the couch and chuckled face down in to the floor.

"It's one o'clock," Olive mentioned, a reference to our lack of sobriety and the appropriateness of Tom's childish behavior. He was suddenly resembling the New Florentine's other drunk, William Zofield.

"Get up Mr. Zofield... excuse me, Mr. Reynolds," I said. Tom did not listen to me so I stood and pulled on his arm to try and get him to sit up, not wanting him to realize what kind of a fool he was being portrayed as in the eye of Olive's lens later on.

"Mr. Zofield is dead," Tom hooted. "Or at least I thought he was until he showed up on this boat. You know, I could have sworn I saw in the paper he died... about two years ago I think."

"You're thinking of Walter Zikosky, the other Brit."

"Who?" Tom asked, dumbfounded.

"Zikosy! The scientist who later turned in to a sci-fi novelist after the war."

"What war?"

"The one in the mid-east."

"Which one?"

"The first one."

"No! Which mid-east?" Tom began laughing uncontrollably. "You know, mid-west, mid-east."

Olive stopped taking pictures and stood still, drolly taken by Tom's antics. Moments later he'd fall asleep on the couch and I would take Olive out on the ship's starboard deck to discuss the same matter I had with Bryan.

"He knows about us," I said brusquely.

"I know. We had an argument about it ten minutes ago. But I think it's for the best that he knows."

"Me too. Even if it's over." I truly was relieved the affair was no longer a secret.

"Over?" Olive questioned. She now had permission to see me and my assertion that anything we'd shared be finished angered her. This was me rejecting her and she could not manage such a setback. "What do you mean it's over Marc?"

"I can't go on having sex with you knowing your husband is in the other room."

"You're insane," she said, angrily clasping her hips and turning away from me. Then under her breath she said, "maybe he'd like to join us." I wasn't supposed to hear the comment and so I didn't ask her what she meant. But now I suspected there to be a greater, more perverse layer to Bryan and Olive's sex life.

In a search for seclusion I found Halston's library to be the ideal place for serenity and reflection, however I was not alone in the room. Giuseppe sat quietly reading at one of the library's desks and nodded at me when I entered, silently welcoming my presence. After meandering around the library and inspecting some of the books, many of which were signed by their authors, I approached Giuseppe to see what he was reading. Previously I'd taken the young man as a dimwit and assumed he'd be reading a comic book sheathed in Jane Austen. As I tried to examine the cover of the book, obscured by his large, working class fingers, he said "Pike Street." He could not have said two more offensive words.

"What page are you on?" I asked.

"432." He only had another 220 to go.

"Do you hate it?"

"No. I very much like the texture of Pike Street."

"Yes. It was printed on very nice paper," I replied daftly. "It is the one fond thing I remember about that book."

"No! The murkiness of the story. You really get a feel for the underbelly of Seattle. When we sailed in to Seattle on Thursday I identified the atmosphere of the town immediately because of your book. How you describe it. 'The confluence of an expanding, aggressive metropolis eroding the roots of a decayed old fishing port.' I love that."

"Something like that," I agreed. His quotation was precise. People who could remember passages like that always frightened me. I thought of them as people who could become master plagiarists if they weren't careful.

"Halston told me this was your worst book," he said without aggression, "but that doesn't say much. Your worst book is better than anything he's written. And I've told him that. It's why we're fighting right now."

"Lover's quarrel?"

"Yes. We're always fighting. We're both very passionate in our beliefs."

I sat down across from Giuseppe to look through some of the decorating and entertainment magazines splayed on the console table, none of which interested me. As I rested my head on the back of Halston's leather couch the thought of taking a nap became appealing. I shut my eyes until the slamming of the library's doors startled me, ending my attempt to doze off.

"Hi Giuseppe," Ashley blared as she entered the library. She waved at me vaguely and smiled, then began examining all the bookshelves around the room. I watched her as she collected about a dozen books in her arms.

"This isn't a bookstore," I kidded.

"I know. Just researching," she said. I then noticed all the books she'd amassed were authored by writers on the ship. Giuseppe noticed the same thing.

"Why are you researching the other writers?" he asked. "Are you writing an article about them?" For a boy toy, Giuseppe was incisive.

"No. Just curious," Ashley lied.

"If you want Olive Snow's third book I have it in my room," Giuseppe offered.

"*The Spring of One's Life?*" Ashley asked.

"That's her second book," he corrected her. "Her third book is *Virginesque.*"

"Whenever you're done with it."

"I'm a slow reader. We'll be to San Francisco by the time I'm done. I'll give it to you later today."

Ashley nodded in accordance and exited with her pile of books.

"Have you read all our books?" I asked Giuseppe.

"Almost. Except for Tom Reynolds's."

"Don't you like Tom's books?" I queried.

"If you've read one Tom Reynolds book you've read them all," he replied, making us both laugh.

"You must be incredibly bored on this boat," I said.

"Yes. And Halston always wants to travel to wherever we are not. So instead of going some place and exploring it we're always just traveling somewhere. He's tired of destinations before we've reached them."

"How long have you known Halston?"

"Three weeks."

Gay men and their relationships had always perplexed me, mostly because of their diversity. In my limited observances of the species I'd seen both men who feasted on as many lovers as they could consume, and in contrast, another kind that spent their lives with only one partner. Never was it safe to assume that all were the ravenous kind so I took a sort of sensitivity to discussing Halston and Giuseppe's relationship.

"How'd you meet Halston?" I asked.

"He was at a party in Santa Barbara."

"I thought you were from Italy."

"I am. I moved to Hollywood when I was 25 to be an actor. Or a model. Or a waiter. Anything. But when I got to Hollywood I found about a million other fools wanting the same jobs I wanted. And I'm not just talking about acting parts. I tried to be a valet and had to compete with ten other boys to get the job. In L.A. you have to audition just to be a dishwasher in a food truck. Made me want to go back home."

"What part of Italy are you from?"

"Antignano."

"That's near Livorno."

"Yes!" he suddenly livened, "you know Italy?" He marked his place in *Pike Street* and slammed the book. He was obviously enthralled to speak to someone who knew anything about his country.

"Yes. It's my adopted home."

"Do you have a place there?"

"No. I am a nomad when I get to Italy. I can never decide where I want to live. Probably in the north. I wrote my last book in Florence."

"Your last book?" Giuseppe asked discontented, thinking by *last* I meant *final* and not previous. "Why'd you stop writing?"

"No. I mean the last book I published," I clarified. He nodded his head, acknowledging his mistake.

"Do you speak Italian?" he asked.

"No. I can only read it. My pronunciation is horrendous."

"Like my English. That's why Hollywood didn't like me."

"I think your English is fantastic."

"Thank you."

"It must be lonely on this ship."

"Yes it is," he said slowly and unwillingly. It was a confession of sorts. I sensed in him a tremendous loneliness. While he was surrounded by the yacht crew and Halston, I could see in Giuseppe that he was away from his home and even further away from where he wanted to be.

"What do you do all day?" I asked.

"Watch movies, read, play games."

"Sex games?" I implied. My sudden directness made Giuseppe bashful and he gaped at me for having asked such a question.

"Sometimes," he said, grinning. "You know Halston very long?"

"Twelve years."

"Were you and him…"

"No. I'm not like that."

"Too bad. I know somebody who likes you very much."

"Who?"

"I can't say."

I took his comment as a humorous, self-effacing flirtation. Giuseppe picked up the copy of *Pike Street*, stood, and exited the library. He impressed me with his adept and brave humor and I knew then there was more to this gigolo than just his charms. He desired everyone and they were allured by his foreign, if not naive ambition for success in America. He probably made a lot of friends in Hollywood, the good and bad kind. Giuseppe was never taken advantage of because as much as one might use him for his beauty and youth (a façade considering he was 29 but could easily pull off 19), it was Giuseppe who'd allowed and controlled the circumstance. He was here on the boat because it was not his destiny but mission within a greater career agenda to network within the players of the arts. One might assume he was using Halston to gct to Bryan Madden in the hopes of putting him in one of his pictures. But after some careful observation of Giuseppe I was well assured he had his eyes fixated on another tycoon of a different industry.

FIDELITY

Ashley Mulberry was barricaded in her bedroom after deciding she'd remain involved with the happenings of the New Florentine. No longer an author or creator, she was now a journalist and documentarian. At first I had been off-put by her charge to examine the dichotomy of the group, but accepted the idea having slept on it. It started to intrigue me on what an outsider's perspective might be and I began to anticipate what her observations could expose.

"Do you realize there isn't one writer from the south on the boat?" Ashley pointed out, sitting at her desk as I shuffled through the books of my colleagues stacked on her dresser.

"Halston is from the south," I said. "Baton Rouge. He won't tell you that, but he is."

"Are you the only one who knows he is from Louisiana?"

"I think so. Giuseppe might know."

"Who?"

"Giuseppe the Italian guy. His lover."

"They're lovers!" Ashley exacerbated.

"How dense can you be?" I mocked. "It doesn't take a genius to figure out Halston is a-"

"I know he's a homosexual. But Giuseppe is so rugged. He doesn't look *that* way at all!"

My presence had completely destroyed Ashley's productivity. She came and sat next to me on her suite's couch and flipped through the pile of books she'd taken from the library.

"You live in San Francisco and have yet to develop the knack for identifying the various archetypes of gay men?" I posed.

"There are no more gay people per capita in San Francisco than there are in Seattle or Los Angeles. It's just an exaggerated myth. Like London's fog or Chicago's wind."

"I don't know Ashley. Last time I was in 'Frisco I sure got a lot of glances," I joked.

"You're conceited. I'm sure they were just staring at the man with his nose in the air."

"It wasn't my nose they were looking at," I laughed suggestively.

"Anyway!" Ashley blasted, wanting to drop the topic, "what is going to happen tonight?"

"At the readings? Nothing at all. Why?"

"You people are so boring. Or I'm just missing the subtleties."

"You're missing it all. Bryan asked me if I was sleeping with Olive."

"What a jerk!"

"But the truth is I was. And I told him that." Ashley feigned shock when I said this.

"Did he punch you?" Ashley was now riled by the hint of scandal.

"No. He was friendly. As if he was relieved to find out she was getting some on the side."

"I can't believe you Marc." She shook her head, "Sleeping with a married woman!"

"You're one to talk! You've been married three times and how many affairs have you had?" The answer to that question is seven.

"It's not called an affair if you're retaliating against your husband!" she declared, slamming shut the copy of Olive Snow's earliest novel, *The Great Oppression*.

"Maybe. But you never did prove any of your *three* husbands to have actually been cheating."

"There may not have been proof," she accepted, "but a woman knows her husband. Amelia must have known about you and Olive." It was a trait of my sister's to revert to the most painful and strenuous time of my life in order to impose reprisal.

"The thing with Olive took place after Amelia. I never cheated on my wife. And if I had I would have told her about it and we would have moved on. The ability to overcome adultery is customary in a strong marriage."

"Strong marriage?" Ashley cackled. "The divorce papers are still being shuffled around law offices as we speak. You're a philandering whore Marc Mulberry. Men like you are beasts."

I did not respond to Ashley's dramatics and instead flipped open Katrin Zofield's modern day classic, *WoManhattan*, to a random page and read:

As LaQuanda lingered her tongue around the Steve's bulbous pink head and massaged his fur covered scrotum with her hands, she thought to herself 'maybe I'm not cut out to be a flight attendant.' But suddenly he groaned, gasped, yelped and squirted all over her server's apron. She then decided she was more than fit to handle both the pilots and life in the skies.

Never had I read any of Katrin's work, merely overhearing that it was salacious, stylized kitsch too raunchy even for *Cosmopolitan* magazine, where she once worked but was famously fired for inappropriate relations with an executive at the company. If there's anything to be learned from reading a book it is that a writer puts his or her soul in to it. In that moment I felt more compelled than ever to get to know Ms. Zofield more closely.

WHORES

To have not been socially monopolized by Halston Levy by the near end of the second day of the cruise was unfamiliar. This was a man who for several years I called my best friend — the only other person who knew I secretly wanted to be a writer and not another cog in the machine. In the yacht's kitchen I found him helping the chef prepare the evening's dinner. It seemed as though no matter how many staff Halston employed, be they chefs, housekeepers, decorators or florists, he was always right alongside them, fussing around attempting perfection. I don't know if he didn't trust them or he felt compelled to help them.

"Sorry Marc, nothing is going as planned," Halston appealed to me as he sliced heirloom tomatoes for a colorful fennel salad. Halston's demeanor had begun to show fluster, a trait unlike his regular, unflappable self. It was evident that a bit of frustration was being alleviated as he sliced the tomatoes.

"It's only dinner," I tried to soothe, "we'll eat anything. I'm sure the chef can handle this." Indeed the chef, who had his own television show, agreed with this statement and became pleasantly insistent Halston banish himself from the kitchen. The two of us would convene in the empty dining room to assemble the dinnerware and décor.

"You're acting aloof," I said.

"I just have things on my mind."

"Are you writing something?" I delicately wondered aloud.

"Sure," he said. I detected a lie. Any previous time in which I asked Halston if he was writing something I'd never heard the word 'sure.' He was a constant promoter, never one to shield attention from his work. He was better than any PR machine money could buy. Always ready to promote his next work, no matter how unfinished it was. Something was the matter.

"What are you writing?" I asked.

"Nothing," he said, miffed. "I'm blocked."

"I brought some laxatives if you-"

"-Marc!" Halston objected to my humor. "I've never been blocked before."

"So! Everybody goes through it."

"No. I mean it. I've always been able to write. Even when I didn't feel like putting something down on the page I could still do it because of my determination. My self-discipline is something I've always admired about myself. It's in fact the only thing I've ever admired about myself. But now I sit down, fully determined, and nothing comes to mind."

"Sir," I called Halston this whenever he began to act rather youthful and naïve, "you've written a lot in the last ten years. Maybe you need a break."

"What are you talking about? My life is one long soirée. Nothing but parties, charities, promotions – it could really get in the way of writing. That is if there was anything to write about."

"No. A *real* vacation. No obligations. This whole lifestyle of yours is a charade made possible by your relentless domesticity. Spend a month in Belize without the boat or the staff of helpers. Don't expect anything, just let it happen. You, Giuseppe, or whoever, and nothing else but the sun and the beach."

"If you knew what you were talking about I'd be fascinated, but you don't."

"God damn it Halston," I popped, "you've become a perfectionist! You host these cruises and parties to impress everyone and I don't know why."

"There is a function to all this." He retaliated, "We have a responsibility to discuss the issues. We are writers - we document history but do not dictate it. To communicate with one another is crucial."

"So call me."

"Fuck Marc!" he finally wailed, heaving a stack of china and silverware on the floor. The shattering commotion was followed by him storming out of the room. He would retreat to his bedroom and issued an announcement via the staff that he would not be attending dinner. This caused the readings to be cancelled

and everyone to stay in their rooms for the rest of the night, or so
we were instructed to do.

"You bastard," Katrin lampooned as I explained the
circumstances of Halston's meltdown. We ate our dinners on the
same table we'd eaten breakfast and I was beginning to feel as
though Katrin and I were living together on the yacht.

"I'm worried about him," I said. "I've never seen him this
unstable. I've never seen him destroy things."

"Maybe you were too abrasive with him," she proposed. I
shook my head in disagreement.

"He's probably the most resilient person I know." I said,
"they don't call him critic-proof for no reason."

"The criticism of journalists as opposed to friends is a very
different kind of scrutiny. Does he have very many friends?" she
asked, insinuating that I might be Halston's only friend.

"He has friends in New York," I disputed. "And lovers in
every attractive port on every continent on the globe. A real true
sailor."

"Any friends outside of publishing and fucking?"

"No," I conceded. Katrin's proposal altered my idea of
Halston, someone I viewed as a lost soul sailing the world looking
for inspiration through beautiful people and friends, now a lonely
older gentlemen clinging to an idea of glamour too unobtainable
for a single person to subscribe too.

"Where are we?" Katrin asked, filling her glass with the last
of the Chateau Fableaux.

"Near Astoria, Oregon... I think."

From the mini fridge I took a bottle of fume blanc from my
own estate and uncorked it. Katrin quickly emptied her glass and
refilled it with the Mulberry and drank that too. It was apparent
she was in a race to become inebriated.

"Your wine is delicious," she said, quaffing the glass, mocking
a true connoisseur. We talked loosely of what we hated about
everyone on the boat until Katrin dropped her dinner napkin
under the table (probably on purpose). This was hysterical to her
and on the journey to recover the piece of linen she found herself

between my legs. At first I thought her to be mimicking one of her trademark Katrin Zofield sex scenes of casual entanglement. Not until she began massaging the crotch of my trousers did I take her actions as serious. This did not yield a reaction of outrage in me as what she was doing began to release some of the most powerful stimulations I'd felt in a long time – a kind of pent sexual compulsion now being coaxed from my pants. My immediate erectness pleased Katrin and it did not take her long unzip my pants and start at it with her mouth. Her directness in fondling me must have pleased her greatly as I watched her laugh between attempts to swallow as much of me as she could and every so often take a sip of wine to lubricate her throat.

Drunkenly we began kissing and groping each other like two fools. The dress she wore was quite long and as I reached up between her legs to remove her panties I discovered she wasn't wearing any. I fingered her briefly and with such a gesture she demanded I return the oral favor already paid to me. Not wanting to work in the dark I stood Katrin up, slipped her dress off, tossed her back on the bed, spread her open and began to devour her. She instructed me to shove my tongue in as far as it would go and I followed suit. Katrin further instructed I make love to her underneath the sheets "in a more conventional way." We humped for not more than ten minutes until she came. As she climaxed she let her roving hands proceed down to my buttocks. This had been previously unexplored territory as far as women went and it resulted in one of the most climatic orgasms I can recall ever having. It was so intense my entire midsection continued to pulse with pleasure for minutes after I climaxed.

"You always do that?" I asked her moments post-orgasm. She knew something most women did not.

"Yes," she said, "I read in a magazine there are as many nerves in the anus as there are in a person's foot."

"Is that a lot?"

"You tell me," she replied with a cutesy shrug immediately followed by a drunken burp.

FASCINATIONS

Thirty-foot sea swells five miles off the coast of Oregon could not keep me from purging prose on to page Sunday morning. I recall waking moments before sunrise and rushing to the computer where I would write for two hours straight, resulting in a manifesto of introspection larger than anything I'd written in a single sitting before. Miraculously, a night of sex had cured my writer's block!

The first duty of business after writing was not to see how Katrin was doing. Afterall, she was still asleep in my bed. Rather I went to the kitchen to find the breakfast the staff was preparing for their boss and offered to take it to him myself. They thought the idea was fantastic considering Halston had confronted most of them in a tizzy the night before and was not on their best side at the moment.

When I rolled the immaculate banquet in to Halston's room he sat up in bed, noticeably entertained by my role playing and began ordering me around like I was one of his servants. Quickly I collected strewn garments and put them in the laundry hamper and lit the pillar candles adorning his table. Giuseppe was nowhere in sight.

"Where's Giuseppe?" I asked, expecting him to be resting next to Halston.

"He doesn't sleep in this room. He sleeps in the staff quarters downstairs."

"Why? I though he was your-"

"Yes, he is my lover. But he insists on living with the crew. He even does the laundry and dishes. Can you believe that?"

"In a way he is like one of your servants."

"He is not a servant! I don't pay him to be here!" Halston was furious that I might imply he had to pay for sex.

"I'm sorry. I'm just confused at these things – I guess you could say I'm very sheltered." He was charmed by this statement and, despite our early quarreling, scuttled out of his giant bed to the table I'd arranged for him. After he sat down I placed his covered breakfast in front of him and lifted the silver dome lid with the same bit of fanfare I'd seen done in pretentious restaurants. What I uncovered was the most devastatingly beautiful and intricate fruit salad, layered in a massive pyramid of melon spheres and berries.

"They really are amazing," I said.

"They're artists, not just chefs."

"I feel like I should take a picture of that thing. It would do a pharaoh proud." I sat down across from Halston to find the staff had brought him the day's *International Herald Tribune*, something I assumed must have been flown in via helicopter from the mainland. I imagined a paperboy manning a helicopter and tossing the day's news on to various yachts as they wandered across the Pacific.

"What's with all the jokes Marc? You're usually so reserved and quiet. Most of the time I have to force you to speak to me."

"You don't like the funny version of me?"

"No. I like it. I'm just curious if there is motivation behind it."

"I don't think so," I replied, somewhat disturbed by his suspicion. "Of all the people on this yacht I must be one of the least motivated. What could possibly be my motivation?"

"I don't know," Halston said just as he decided to perforate the pyramid's western raspberry flank to reveal an interior structure of waffle hidden inside. "No one is who they seem anymore."

"What do you mean?"

"God damn it!" he suddenly blasted, not at me but at himself. He pushed his breakfast away and began to sob. "I don't know. I make these statements but I have no idea where they come from."

"Are you going crazy?"

"Most likely. My father went crazy." He halved the fruit pyramid making a catastrophic mess. He had no respect for the intricate beauty he devoured.

"Your father was accidentally electrocuted and became paralyzed."

"I have cancer," he then stated, rather as a question than an affirmation.

"You have cancer?" I asked for clarification, "What kind?"

"I don't know. But I could. Brain cancer most likely although it could have started someplace else. Like the lungs or the prostate. Do you still smoke?"

"Yes. But not that much."

"Can I have one of your funny little Grecian cigarettes?" He held out his open palm, anxious for me to give him one.

"No. And they're Italian. Besides, cancer patients shouldn't smoke," I riled him.

"I don't have cancer. I just feel as though something is happening within me. I've become fascinated with the most ordinary things."

"Like what?"

"I can't tell you. You'll think it's ridiculous."

"No I won't, tell me," I coaxed softly, still trying to soothe the frazzled man.

Halston stood from the table and motioned for me to follow him to his private study, a separate and smaller room between his bedroom and the grand library. Inside this room he showed me an extravagant collection of model cars, each no larger than a shoebox, all of them of vintage models from the mid 1940s and prior.

"Did you build these?" I asked.

"Yes. This is my cancer. I don't know what's wrong with me. The only thing I want to do is build these stupid little cars. Some of them I don't even like." No matter how hard I try to concentrate on writing my mind always returns to these toys.

I then noticed in his display case a convertible Alfa Romeo roadster precisely the same model as the one I owned. Inside the car was a little figurine that looked not unlike myself, wearing a black sweater, pinstripe pants, and smoking a tiny sliver of a cigarette.

"You devil!" I chaffed him with laughter. It was a tribute to have been immortalized so glitteringly.

"I'm like a child with these cars. Never have I been interested in automobiles before. In fact I've always been morally at odds with the internal combustion engine."

"How'd you get hooked on them?"

"Giuseppe. He bought a couple in Santa Barbara before we left. This is after I told him how boring yachting can be. Now he's moved on to my old flame, literature, and I'm the child assembling the toys."

"They're not toys," I rebuffed, "they're beautiful works of art."

"Put any spin on it you want," he said, then pointed out a logo on one of the unassembled boxes that read 'recommended for ages eight through fourteen.' "I've begun the death procession."

"Shut up. It's just a hobby, that's all." I contemplated telling him how I'd spent ages 27 through 31 collecting bowling trophies from thrift stores, having been fascinated by the golden plastic monuments of mediocrity, but instead decided to let him marinate in his despair.

We went back in to his bedroom where I watched him finish his breakfast and he chatted to me about how he thought his newfound hobby was actually a case of transference. Halston believed the only reason he was interested in model cars was because Giuseppe had taken an interest in them. He confessed to me his forbidden love for Giuseppe and I questioned how it could be considered prohibited as they were having sex regularly, if not multiple times a day.

"The last thing in the world you're supposed to do with your houseboy is fall in love with him," Halston explained. "Sex on a fire escape... or blowjobs on the beach, that's all normal. But to fall in love is just so morbid. I'm a weak, weak man."

I blushed at Halston's frankness. He picked up on my discomfort and changed subjects.

"I hear you're writing again," he said.

"Yes," I sang. "Like never before."

"Is it the sex?"

"What sex?" I asked. He had no way of knowing about me and Katrin. Unless there were hidden "security" cameras in the bedrooms.

"Katrin told me. You know we're attached at the handbag."

"Somehow I forgot," I said, having overlooked the fact Katrin and Halston had been friends almost as long as he and I had. Then I recalled they'd met at a gallery opening in New York just after Halston hit the bestsellers list with his debut novel, *Locker Room*. Together they were a miraculous if not cliché pair, he being the flaming homosexual arbiter of fashion and home décor, and she the fabulous urban ingénue addicted to designer apparel.

RHETORIC

"God damn! It reeks of sex in here!" burst Ashley as she entered my bedroom to say good morning.

"How can you smell the sex through the cigarette smoke?" I asked.

"It's some very pungent sex!"

"Pungent? *Really?*"

"I can't believe you. Sleeping with Olive again after telling Bryan of the affair. That takes balls." Her eyes swerved across the room looking for some physical evidence of the act. I can only imagine her reaction if she found a bottle of lubricant or a set of anal beads.

"I'm not sleeping with Olive," I corrected.

"Then who was the sex with? The only other female is… Katrin!"

"Sssh!" I hushed, "she's only two doors down."

"You whore! I can't believe you!" Apparently I sullied her idea of Katrin, who Ashley wrongly presumed to have good taste in men.

"Well I'm bored, there's nothing else to do on this yacht!" I bolstered. "Eat, sleep, write - I get tired with just those three activities."

"I thought you guys were supposed to be intellectuals but all you do is sleep with each other. It's absolutely profane!"

"Yes. But don't you think it's fantastic material for your book?" This statement completely altered Ashley's take on things. Now the purpose of the cruise appeared to be not an orgy of the minds but of the bodies.

"Do they know about each other?" she asked, now captivated by the details of each infatuation.

"You mean, do they know I've slept with both of them?" This was a concern I hadn't ever had in my life. "Probably not. But who cares? We're all very open minded individuals. Except for Tom Reynolds, I think he is religious. A catholic maybe."

"Are you joking!" she slandered, "the man practically groped me."

"What are you talking about?" I asked, suddenly engrossed in her affairs just as she was in mine.

"Last night at dinner," she feigned discretion.

"But dinner was cancelled," I replied.

"Yes. But the four of us - Olive, Bryan, Tom and me - met for dinner in the front lounge area. We're not prisoners on this ship. I certainly won't be told when and where to eat!"

"Why didn't you tell me?"

"I assumed you were busy."

"I probably was," I reconsidered. "He *groped* you?"

"Yes. We were dancing. You know like they do in movies… how people used to when they held each other. Anyway, he was showing me how to do a dance called the fox hop."

"Fox *trot*," I corrected.

"Whatever! Anyway he was leaning on me and he put his hands on my ass."

"And you were offended?"

"No. It was quite unexpected, yet arousing. I don't mind that he's 25 years older than me. He's aged very well."

"And you like older men," I pointed, now an established fact she cringed at when verbalized.

"Yes. But the move was just very presumptuous. He's married and I'm in a relationship."

"With a philanthropist, I know. But now you're a big, sleazy whore on a boat. The novel can be called 'The Philanderer and the Philanthropist.'" We both chuckled at the title. "I can tell you wanted it. The emptiness of the open sea does that to people."

"I've never felt hornier!" she quickly acknowledged.

"So hop on it. What happens on the New Florentine stays on the New Florentine."

"Fuck you Marc, this isn't Las Vegas. And even it were, I can't have sex with Tom Reynolds."

"Why not?"

"I'm not that kind of girl. I could never cheat on someone. It's not in me."

"It's not in you *yet!*" I joked, prompting her to slap my arm. She threw herself on the chaise lounge and clasper her brow.

"Ashley," I finally surmised, "in this age where oral sex isn't even considered sex, I think you should reconsider what a little innocent flirting can do for the spirit."

"I was just thinking…" Ashley paused, then tattled in a lower tone, "if I were to sleep with anyone on the yacht it would be Bryan. He's absolutely gorgeous."

I approached the chair and sat next her.

"We goddamn Mulberries are nothing but home-wreckers." She and I both laughed at the statement and I could tell from her amusement that an attempt to seduce Bryan Madden wasn't far from her mind.

Not a moment passed until the telephone began ringing. I answered it to find Halston requesting mine and Ashley's presence in the library.

"We're wanted," I said, tapping Ashley on the knee.

"I'm not going."

"You'll need to take notes for your book," I remarked.

"I can't sell this book. You're all so vain and petty. You're all just children heralded as great minds who've become so convinced by your cheering critics that what you do is of value. Not one of you has a true insight or initiative. It's as if you're all just swimming in the beauty of your surroundings, confident you're part of the splendor. I have not heard one of you mention the new mediums."

"What new mediums?" I asked.

"The Internet and social media."

"What about them?" I asked, admittedly in a dismissive, elitist tone.

"What's your opinion of their contributions to the downfall of the printed word?"

"Downfall of the printed word?" I restated, unsure she'd chosen the correct term.

"Yes!" she sat up to face me. "Your obsolescence," Ashley then gasped at her own assertion for extra drama. "Books are dead. Nobody reads anymore."

"You don't know what you're talking about," I affirmed. We then took our conversation in to the library where it was quickly beaten and strangled.

"What kind of a dumb fucking cunt are you?" William Zofield blistered Ashley. "Book sales are off the charts in Europe and even here in America. You're out of touch lady!"

"Yes, book sales are up," Ashley allowed, then countered, "but not fiction. Sales of literature are down thirty percent in the last ten years. You've all seen a dwindling of shelf space. The dominance novels once had is quickly being eroded by nonfiction, biography, and even the dreaded self-help."

The term 'self-help' was blasphemous in my circle and was met with discomfort. Halston wanted the dramatics to end and offered everyone a stiff cocktail. It surprises people that someone such as myself, a winemaker, does not enjoy being intoxicated. In my younger days I'll admit there was nothing more fun than getting smashed and having a rollicking time out on the town. I hazily recall my late twenties as nothing but a period of drinking, and chasing women and cabs. But these days, the ones shallowly buffering the 40th year of my life, I no longer crave intoxication. There is nothing I wish to be distracted from, not even the antics of my sister and her clashes with my friends. The trauma of unfiltered reality is more than any writer needs in order to feel inspired.

"You're only saying this because you're the only author of a nonfiction piece on this boat," I harpooned Ashley. This would be the first time I'd confront her about her recently released book whose main character was a flat, buffoonish caricature of myself.

"What are you talking about?" she gasped with loosely fabricated astonishment.

"He's talking about that horrendous book of yours dear," Katrin reproached her, saving me the trouble. For Ashley to be vilified by Katrin Zofield, the woman she epitomized and emulated, came as a devastation to her. This was her goddess telling her the work she'd labored over for six months - a relatively short time to write a novel - was futile, if not worthless.

"You are all asses! I hate all of you! I'm going to my room!" These were the final words of Ashley for the day as she pranced off and left only solace in her wake. The group then broke off in to several little tribes to discuss every piquant issue imaginable (Republicans, pop music, the rise of the interstate off-ramp casino, fringe theater). I found myself in a pleasant nook of the library with William Zofield who'd taken a sudden curiosity in my lifestyle. Initially I was at unease, thinking Katrin may have told him of our newfound relations.

"What is the name of the town you live in?" he questioned.

"There is no name. Its unincorporated Island County. The closest landmark is Ebey's Landing."

"Land must be expensive on that island."

"For its proximity to the city it's fairly economical. You can still get a waterfront acre for less than a million."

"That is very reasonable."

Our conversation continued jovially. We would talk of everything except our writings (a glorious retreat from a worn topic), including his daughter Katrin's upbringing by her mother, Sarah Smith, a forgotten American poet who he met in New York City and who died just eight years after Katrin was born. William told me of the difficulties of taking a child born and raised primarily in America and moving them to a London suburb.

"I've never seen someone as furious as she was when I told her we were moving to England."

"Why'd you move?"

"I couldn't handle New York. It was too distracting. I could never work. But Katrin feasts on distraction. The commotion drives her in to introspection whereas it only draws me out of it."

"I'm the same way. If I know there's something other than writing I can be doing then I'll go do it. And I don't know why, I used to be so focused."

"It's senility." William explained, "It starts early in our type – the thinkers. We can easily disguise it as idealism and stubbornness, but we know what it really is. The brain begins to deteriorate. The very tool we use to mold our craft begins to break down."

I did not disagree with William as what he was illustrating was something I'd been suspecting in myself for several years. My mind was leaving me. No longer did it function as rapidly and efficiently as it once did. I look back and now consider its functional zenith to be around the time I turned thirty. However, William's notion of the aging mind came as a paradox to my newest experiences in writing and composition. I was putting on paper sentences structured and aligned countered to what I'd been trained in college. Perhaps my mind was not discarding the ability to invent but the customary technique in doing so, like loosening a restraint.

"Forgive me if I sound naïve, but is it possible the deterioration is actually a neuroses and not a physical decomposition?" I asked William.

"Precisely! It is not the brain tissue which erodes but the operative structure of the brain. Call it the programming. Over time it eliminates all form of creation and experimentation, reassembling itself primarily for survival and essential functioning. Maybe it's a device for efficiency. I can't endure the torture of dealing with agents and publishers in this new condition."

"You still write?"

William hesitated to answer this and instead motioned for the cocktail steward to refill his glass.

"Of course I do," he finally said. This was a revelation. I became inquisitive of his judgment to tell me of it. It had been the conclusion of his own family that he'd stopped working long ago. William added, "It's the only thing I can do anymore."

"Are you going to publish?" I asked.

"Absolutely not!" he blasted. "A cow is much more useful before it's taken to market." I didn't grasp his analogy and was relieved to hear him elaborate. "I've proven myself commercially.

I haven't published in decades yet I still outsell many new and celebrated writers. Now when I create stories they are for me."

"And you're satisfied with that?"

"I don't know," he replied, partially dumbfounded. It felt good to ask a question he didn't see coming. "I suppose I've never been satisfied with a published work I've written, so in a way it doesn't matter."

"I wouldn't be satisfied," I said. "Often I'll dread sending something to my publisher but in the end all the *butchering* they do is for the best."

"Why concern yourself with that now? You have food to eat. Why not just wait all the nonsense out?" His question was rhetorical and made to deride my theory on a publisher's contribution to my work. But one last statement by William would haunt me as it was both prophetic and bold: "Just remember Marc that even the most persuasive publisher can't convince a dead man to alter his masterwork."

BIRDS OF A FEATHER

Sunday night was delightfully uneventful yet stimulating. Katrin and I decided to become nudist hermits in my bedroom. After an hour of foreplay and making love she began proofing and critiquing some copy for the magazine she worked at. I would continue my work with the fetus' autobiography. There is something about nudity that really contributes to my work. The feeling of being naked provides a fluidity of non-restraint to the page that is not there when I am clothed. When I am literally naked it enhances the figurative exposure I'm examining on the page. Not only is my appreciation of one's own frailty heightened but also the notion of humility. To examine my body, a corpse now reluctantly showing its age, sagging where it used to stand rigid and where once wholesome looking skin was is now dotted with sun damage, a man can only get away with a hint of vanity in his writing. This hindsight of aging has given much depth to my new story. This living thing inside its womb knows of the inevitable rotting it must witness. It is wary of being born. It flirts with self-termination, rejection of life, of permanent isolation. If the fetus knew what it would have to endure in the succession known as life, would it choose to never be birthed? If one could preview their life before being dealt it would earth's inhabitants be greatly reduced?

"Katrin?" I asked the lounging proofreader, "If you could be reborn as someone else would you chose to live your life again? Make any changes?"

"Absolutely not!" she declared. "I'm often bewildered by my good fortune. Life is nothing but bliss. I was born in to money, have a famous last name, live in a fantastic city in an unrivaled country, and have made myself very successful. I travel more than I could have ever imagined and if it weren't for the magazine, my life would be one great big leisure pageant. Not only that, have you noticed the toilet seats?"

"No. What about them?"

"They're heated."

Katrin's veneer of bliss was transparent to me. Beneath her gleaming shroud confidence was a woman experiencing tremendous personal anguish. The apparent decline of her father was maddening to her. To Katrin, William was the ultimate hero. He was the man who'd saved her from her self-destructive mother, a woman who'd die of suicide after a famous battle with alcoholism, the entire downfall documented in her many lauded but belligerent works, and who was too weak to fight off the breast cancer she'd been diagnosed with just a month prior to taking her life.

William was a domestic pioneer in the way he brought up Katrin, aiding her in becoming the epitome of female success and independence she now symbolized to many professional modern women. Katrin's many friends in elementary and high school had been intrigued by her father, who before it was commonplace, fulfilled both the maternal and paternal roles of a parent by packing her lunches, washing the laundry, and managing a gleaming home, paid for by his career as a heralded and envied novelist.

William and Katrin would have a falling out when she made the decision to attend college at Columbia instead of Oxford, his alma mater. A proud Englishmen, William felt Katrin was rejecting Britain and its hidebound ways for America, the country which he blamed for corrupting her mother. William did not hate America, rather he viewed it as an over privileged child who'd been given a massive trust fund and now bullied and pouted its way through civilization. It would only be fitting that Katrin would come in to her own feeble inheritance from her mother's estate not long before leaving London for New York, a city she worshipped and praised endlessly in front of him as if to taunt him.

Considered to be a heretic by her father, Katrin would make it in New York writing witty urban tales about idealist young women making it in the city alone. She would become a published author at the age of 23, a year before graduating from college.

The media and critics loved her peculiar heritage and not one brief bio about her went without citing her notorious parents and the legacy she was now helping to affix to the Zofield name. As Katrin's stature in the publishing industry grew it would push William further in to anonymity. Before Katrin published her first collection of tales readers had clamored for William's next work, a project he'd put on hold in order to raise his daughter. Now they no longer craved his words. He'd been replaced by his own kin.

After Katrin's ascendance, William would enter an era of isolation. Unnoticed, he would move from his beloved home in Bloomsbury to a more sprawling and practical estate in the north of Hampstead Heath just past Highgate. There he would resettle in a posh, secluded mansion and take up cooking, archery, and hosting small parties only scholars were invited to. No longer would he be regarded as a writer but someone who used to write. Those who'd known of Zofield as a great writer would begin dying off and after twenty years of silence, most anyone who was not involved in the study of modern literature had forgotten his name or came of age in his daughter's era. Not even Katrin would attempt to rediscover his wit and distinctive perspective. She was a career girl in America, too obsessed with her own self-improvement and prestige to take notice of her father, the national treasure of England. It was in this respect I knew Katrin's father better than she did.

Katrin had continued to review magazine copy as I hesitated at interrupting her work, then recalled we were all supposed to be enjoying ourselves and each other's company, not emulating the tasks of our work lives.

"Do you ever regret the relationship you and your father have?" I asked.

"Yes," she said. "We're both so stubborn. I'm certainly his daughter in that manner. But it's not as if we fight, we just don't have much in common."

"Why don't you ever visit him?"

"I don't know," she began to speculate, "I just feel so sorry for him. He could have been so great and it kills me to see him wasting away."

"Could have been great?" I argued. How she didn't know of her father's standing in the literary world baffled me. "He accomplished more in his time than many of the people on this boat. As for wasting away? He's in his seventies. Why do you say that like it's his fault?"

"It's just my sick work ethic. If I see someone not working I think they're ineffectual, you know, taking up space."

"Would you say your mother was clean?"

"Yes, *immaculate* actually. Living with her was like boot camp. I remember the first thing I did when I woke up in the morning was make my bed. I wasn't allowed to go to the bathroom or eat breakfast until it was made."

"And she made you do many chores?"

"Yes. Everyday once I returned home from school I would do my homework and then spend about two hours doing house work. We didn't have a television so it was either do chores or read. I didn't care much for reading at the time."

"Are you afraid that if you stop working you will die?"

"No. I feel rewarded when I complete my work. To me, work, especially creative work like this, it is the most fulfilling because it impacts the lives of so many women."

"You think fashion magazines enhance the way women live their lives?"

"Yes I do. I know they do. And only a misogynist would ask such a thing. Why all these questions?"

"I'm just learning things about people and it interests me why they make the decisions they do."

After placing her work on the couch, Katrin came to the desk where I was seated and straddled me with her naked body. She was not dominating me, rather gesturing for me to hold her, which I did.

"Do you know your parents?" she asked me.

"No. They're gone."

"How'd they go?"

"Car accident when I was in college."

"I'm so sorry."

"Don't be. Things happen like that."

She stopped talking. We moved to the bed and lay with each other. It was never my intention to share personal stories or sentiments with her. I think we both anticipated our affair to end when we reached San Francisco. Exchanging opinions would have been a redundancy fulfilled only through obligation. But the way she held me was not like you hold a disposable lover. She clang to me with virile attachment, grasping my torso as if she were dangling from the side of a tall building and feeling the tug of gravity far beneath her.

"You're suffocating me," I said, as politely as one can in such a circumstance.

She loosened her grasp and sat up in the bed.

"What are we doing?" she asked.

"What do you mean? We're going to sleep."

"No. We're screwing and having a good time."

"Yes, we do that too. Is there something wrong?"

"I don't know. I can't tell if you like me, you never look me in the eyes. Are you just using me?"

This did not sound like the Zofield of temporal Manhattan; the permanently single, man-eating modern woman of Fifth Avenue who disposed of men like she would a used tampon. There in my bed was a whiney, needy, fragile girl of a woman pouting because, despite being naked in bed with me, felt rejected. She wanted to talk when I just wanted to sleep. And unlike her illusory characters in her wildly successful, so-called highly autobiographical books, she did care what I thought of her. Not since witnessing the enormous size of my chateau had she stopped fantasizing what it would be like to snag me. To have conquered Marc Mulberry, the great bachelor and eternal man-boy, would be a prominent notch in her bedpost. The thought of her using me to accomplish a public relations ambition did not abhor me. If she was going to let herself be ensnared by the lures of my monetary accomplishments then I was determined to benefit from it. The more I had sex with Katrin the more I was able to write. And at that time in my life the only thing better than having so much sex was writing more than I ever believed I could in such a brief epoch during an event as sordid as a boat trip down the West Coast.

ECSTASY

The first full day in the waters off Oregon were met with a flare of heat. When I opened the doors of my bedroom that went out to the deck it let the new, sultry atmosphere of the sea in, beckoning a complete transformation in the mood of everyone aboard. This smooth, warm Monday morning became a drastic juxtaposition to the previous day of unexpected gusts and momentary chills.

Anticipating the blissful weather, Halston had arranged for the ship to stop just off the coast of Agate Beach near Newport. The nine of us would sail to the shore, in what they called a dinghy (a petite yacht in itself named Il Pitti that lived inside the hull of the New Florentine), to discover a picnic breakfast had been coordinated by some local merchants and the New Florentine staff. The casualness of the early meal was greatly needed. Leaving the formality of the yacht warranted smiles from everyone, even William, who was enchanted by the unforeseen paradise.

The layers of clothing we once all huddled beneath began to be shed. After the meal Halston devised an expedition to the nearby lighthouse. The mood during this hike was completely cheerful and upbeat, as if this had been the first time anyone of us had experienced such serenity. The lighthouse we chased sat graciously perched on a small jute of boulders forming a peninsula separate from the contrasting sand of the beach, its revolving light no longer the magnitude it once was but now a cosmetic showpiece that dimmed at night so it did not disturb its millionaire neighbors.

At the lighthouse everyone dispersed to find their own vantage on the high bank. Some would scale the staircase to the tower's pinnacle and shout greetings down to those on the ground and even to the New Florentine bobbing out in the Pacific. I would conduct my search for privacy on the trails running the banks which ran the perimeter of the bluff on which the lighthouse stood beaming. Looking for sea life, and hoping to collect a starfish, I sauntered down to where the water hit the rocks and found Bryan Madden alone, seated on the wet boulders staring out at the vast blue horizon. He did not notice my presence, the sound of my footsteps muffled by the wrestling waters. The way his body sat, his head drooping and his arms grasping small pebbles and tossing them in to the ocean angrily, I could only assume Bryan to be sulking. Just as I decided to leave he turned to me, almost startled to find that his isolation had been entreated upon.

"Marc," he said, his face crumpled in sadness.

"Bryan, are you alright?" I asked.

"I'm just a little queasy. Side-effects of the sea life I guess. How are you?"

I took a seat next Bryan on the rocks, reassured he was not annoyed by my company.

"Things are good. I've been writing," I replied.

The sun was radiant and a gentle wind became the perfect compliment to the dewy atmosphere of the sultry shore. I leaned my back up against the wall of rocks and watched the waves crash in to the bluff not far from our feet. The sky was bright and clear and I closed my eyes briefly until I felt the unexpected pressure of Bryan's lips on mine, his hand suddenly on my knee.

"What are you doing?" I asked, pushing him away.

"I don't know," he said, his expression now lost. "I'm sorry!"

Bryan stood up with humiliation, his eyes signaling regret. Just as he began to leave a large tumbling wave collided with the rocks in front of us, shooting in to the sky and over us, then splashed down in a cool blast causing Bryan to lose his balance. Not wanting him to fall on the rocks and hurt himself I quickly reached for his arm and steadied him. Consequently, this move triggered me to fall on to him and our bodies were for a moment on top of one another. Instantly my mind rejected the disposition but my body failed to react with such disdain. Feeling his warm, sturdy body beneath mine was cumbersome but not repulsive. And so I laughed at the mishap, as did Bryan, and we failed to stand and would let another wave crash in to the rocks and rain down on us. At this moment I could feel Bryan's reaction to our pose, a stiffening in the khaki shorts he wore, as well as an unexpected stirring in my own. This startling arousal prompted me to find my balance and stand up.

"Marc!" Bryan called after me as I ascended the trail towards the lighthouse. At once I was running from him. For a man to arouse me was astonishing, especially a man I once loathed so intensely. But the nerves which now prompted me to sprint up the trail were not only fear but also excitement. I had discovered a new facet of enticement in myself. A man could arouse me just as a woman could.

At the top of the trail in the sandy clearing of the lighthouse grounds I found the three women of the cruise laughing at me. Thinking they could have possibly witnessed what happened from the lighthouse's pinnacle I began to panic. But my fear was doused when Ashley reprimanded me. "You're soaked, you moron!"

"Yes, a giant wave..." I paused to catch my breath.

I was quick to escape the scene by having one of Halston's staff take me back out to the New Florentine in the dinghy with the excuse that I wanted to change in to dry clothes. But I would not return to the shore where everyone frolicked. I'd retreat to the comfort of my bedroom to sit at the desk and begin to write. That was until I found what I wanted to purge to page had fled my mind. Not an hour prior I had considered a whole new chapter... something about the fetus calling its parents via telephone, an idea I now found ridiculous. I then concluded the brilliance of the chapter permanently unrealized and replaced by impulses of disgust and regret, not toward the story but for Bryan. His inclination to kiss me and the resulting sensations of paradox still rippling through my nerves had destroyed everything creative or compelling already fostered in them. I'd been dealt a violent strike. I then wondered if he'd meant to stun me.

My hands were shaking as I poured myself a glass of water. I went to the window to smoke and calm myself but it would take more than nicotine and the view to do that.

I sat on the bed and asked myself why I was so shaken. I had no answer. My cure to writer's block before had been to make love to Katrin. So I stated right then, "I'll fuck Katrin when she gets back!" and all was calm and fine with me for that moment. It was then I noticed a svelte manuscript sitting on my nightstand with a note on top of it. The note read:

Mr. Mulberry, I apologize in advance if this offends you, but I would like to ask for your opinion. I have penned my first novel and I fear it is gibberish compared to any work as great as yours. People have read it and have told me it is good... but they are just people, they're not authors. We are not much more than strangers but to me there could be no estimation of my work more highly regarded than yours.

Ringraziarlo, Giuseppe

Beneath the letter was *Ecstasy*, Giuseppe's manuscript. For a moment I began to wonder if everyone on the boat was an author. It then occurred to me that everyone was.

Whenever someone asks me to read a draft I become reluctant, explaining I have a horrible eye for catching mistakes and even a more rancid ability to distinguish melodrama from sincerity in text. I'm a dreadful reader. But I did not decline *Ecstasy*, for its first page was able to seize my attention immediately. It began: "It's not every day you rape a nun." Following this was the tale of a Venetian priest who attempts to condemn America's global culture of sex and profanity by becoming a writer for an Italian newspaper. He travels to Rome to witness the concert of a great American pop star during which he fortuitously consumes an ecstasy tablet and begins a spree of rape, brutality, and sexual exploration. The novel ends just as the liberated priest flies the hijacked pop star's jet into the Eiffel Tower. The novel was brilliant, over-the-top escapist fun I would read all 250 pages of in a mere two hour stint. Like all drafts the book wasn't perfect, having minor mechanical lapses and sporadic, random language problems, such as using Italian adjectives in places he did not know of appropriate English ones.

But even with the errors I was floored by his aptitude. Giuseppe, the alleged wannabe actor and freelance male hooker had suddenly become my favorite author on the boat. His glib and outlandish narrative had been able to distract me from my own anxious state, and I was grateful.

THE POSSESSION OF YOUTH

The glee and whimsy derived by leaving the New Florentine for the shore had been brought back aboard by my fellow travelers as they returned to the boat for lunch. No longer were we a group of clashing egos but a collection of eager vacationers basking in the newfound freshness of mutual appreciation. It was even possible that some of us were nostalgic and captive of the remaining time as the trip would end in just two days. Contrarily, I was finding the isolation of the ship to be numbing and could not wait to reach San Francisco so I could promptly take a taxi to the airport.

Discovering Giuseppe to be a more than capable writer made me eager to meet with him to discuss his work. No longer was he resigned to the corner in social situations. He was mingling and laughing with the others, a sign he was warming up to the old guard he probably revered, if not for their writing ability, their commercial successes. Yet when I found him, chatting gaily with Katrin about the red light district of Amsterdam, he hushed me when I began to talk about his dazzling novel. The rest of the writers were in the midst of a discussion about America's two major artistic identities: the Old Coast of the east and the New Coast of the west. Anything to do with the interior workings of the United States captivated Giuseppe, and for the first time, William Zofield. It crossed my mind that in the last decade Europeans had become much more concerned about America's global influence than Americans.

"When America is not busy looking at itself as one giant, glorious edifice of perfection and superiority," William started, "and it's severed in to two opposing sums, the dissimilarities begin to materialize and it's a wonder the whole thing stays together."

"You mean it's a miracle we've only had one civil war?" Katrin prompted.

"Yes. Considering that the empires of the Pacific Coast, Midwest, Greater New England and the South are so unique in culture, economy, and values."

"Other than their geography, what's so different between the regions?" Giuseppe questioned. "I can't tell Houston from Denver... St. Louis from Portland... Minneapolis from Atlanta."

"The West is so austere compared to the South or Northeast," Tom started. "There is a history of very little to no warfare out here, other than the expected battles between natives and the settlers. It's one of the few regions in the world that has such a claim."

"Yes. The country's two great civilizations, Los Angeles and New York, could not be more divergent," Halston informed us.

"Neither could their people," I stated. "On the Old Coast creeds live in colonies. The Latinos, Italians, blacks, and Irish maintain their own distinct neighborhoods where they live isolated from each other. In a city like Seattle you have a true melting pot. There are no chunks in the stew, it's a broth! Every neighborhood is diverse in color, defined mostly by economic standing, not predetermined characteristics like race. The same goes for Vancouver, Portland, and San Diego... they're not the most diverse of cities but their well-stirred."

"In the past ten years of living in New York I have witnessed a sort of exodus." Katrin said, "People leave the city for the West Coast, or as you call it, the New Coast, and are never heard of again. It's as if they've joined the witness protection program."

"And as for religion, it's invisible!" Halston affirmed. "The New Coast is a secular paradise. Where else can a black Jewish quadriplegic Iraq War veteran transvestite roam freely in her motorized chair?"

"The Ile-de-France," William answered.

"Just as long as they're not Arab," Olive countered. "Then they'll be asked to remove their head scarf."

Accusations of American imperialism were offloaded by some in the group while others laughed at the calamity. I paid no mind to the revived backbiting and recalled some of the most succulent passages from Giuseppe's novel so I could give him a thorough recap of what I enjoyed most. But in the presence of Halston he did not want to discuss his work and acted out of an almost embarrassed nature when he insisted I speak to him about the book in private. So I sat there and listened to the group continue to pick to pieces the 300-million-plus people of the United States.

"If you ask a New Yorker where their ancestors are from," Ashley explained, "they'll probably tell you something along the lines of Ireland or Italy. If you ask a San Franciscan where their ancestors are from they'll likely say Pennsylvania or Ohio."

Just before dinner when each of the group's members were getting ready in their bedrooms I found Giuseppe smoking on the boats rear deck. I lit up one of my own and asked him why he seemed to be ashamed of his novel, then reassured him I was not about to criticize it. But just by mentioning the book he became fidgety and hurried, quickly finishing his cigarette and lighting another. With this nervous energy his English deteriorated and he resorted to using many Italian words, most said so quickly I did not understand what he was saying.

"Are you ashamed to be a writer?" I asked him.

"No. It's not that. But I have a purpose on the boat."

"Are you a gigolo?" I asked, not in order to deride but to help illustrate that Giuseppe's own career was just as important as Halston's. To both be writers wouldn't be a competition but a shared enlightenment.

"No. He does not pay me."

"So what do you owe him? Why sacrifice your talent?"

"He doesn't like me writing," he said as he poured himself a glass of red wine.

"Fuck him," I said, "you can't avoid doing what you enjoy because your lover doesn't like it. It's not as if you're doing anything wrong. They're just words on a page."

"Is it not selfish?" he asked.

"You're too Italian. Here in America the self comes first. Trying to please everyone is fruitless."

"Fruit-*less*?" he sought clarification.

"It means to be without success," I illuminated.

"I don't understand how these words work. Fruitless should mean without fruit but it means without success? It's like tireless. It should mean without tires but it means without fatigue."

"You're very astute. How long have you been speaking English?"

"Since nine years old. But I didn't become fluent until high school."

"You must have taken more in college."

"I didn't go to college."

"Why not?"

"I didn't need to. Actors aren't taught how to act," he said stiffly.

"Some are," I said. "But I'm not sure you're an actor. I'm convinced you're going to make it as a storyteller."

"Did someone teach you how to write?" he asked softly.

"Yes. I went to the University of Washington."

"Is that a good school?"

"It's not yet Stanford, but it's getting there."

"Who taught you the most?"

"Charles Dickens," I uttered after a moment's contemplation.

"He's dead."

"Yes. But his work remains," I feebly countered.

"So does Marlon Brando's," Giuseppe quickly shot back.

"Can you learn how to act from just watching movies?" I asked. "I thought it was more mental than that."

"Why should it be? It's acting, not mind surgery."

"Brain surgery," I corrected.

"That's right. Sorry."

"Did you ever read *A Tale of Two Cities*?"

"No. I hate old books. And books that take themselves too seriously. Everyone told me Proust was the greatest French writer and so I bought one of his big fat books. Then I read it and I thought it was boring. Poor France. Who cares what cookies taste like?"

"What contemporary books do you like?"

"I don't know. I read *Nineteen-Eighty-Four* not long ago. I like those books that take place in reality but it's slightly altered just enough to be frightening. Is *Nineteen-Eighty-Four* a modern book?"

"No. It was written decades ago. But if you liked it you should read *The Handmaid's Tale*."

Just then Halston accompanied us on the desk. By his facial expression I conjured he was amused to see his lover and longtime friend getting along so ardently.

"Hello boys," Halston said. "Orchestrating a mutiny out here?"

"Yes. We're bored as hell," I said.

Lost in deep introspection or possible avoidance, Giuseppe did not say anything and when Halston put his arm around him there became a discomfort in his pose, as if the arm was wrapped in barbed wire. Could it be, I wondered, that Giuseppe was using Halston for as many thrills as Halston was utilizing Giuseppe? Usually the young, forgotten, inexperienced men who wonder on to this ship looking for adventure find the malice and heartache they believe to have renounced on the shore has accompanied them in disguise in the form of the miserable Halston, but also in abundance, as time, so precious and rare in the life of a middle-class commoner, is suddenly all one has out on the sea. One day is a lifetime of banal deliberation.

"Halston, did you know Giuseppe has written a book?"

Giuseppe took his vacant gaze off the ocean's horizon in order to glare at me. I was an ardent believer that a lover's quarrel should be left in the arena of the relationship and innocent friends and bystanders, like I, should be left out of such matters.

"It's very entertaining," I added.

"Yes, I've seen him around, writing things down and making notes," Halston reflected. "And sometimes he'll be typing on the computer. He pretends to be writing an email to his family or something else, but I know what he's been doing."

"Have you read it?" I asked.

"No. He keeps all his belongings in a locked trunk and is very careful to never leave anything lying around."

"What kind of a relationship do you have?" I asked tactfully. "Halston, do you even know what he aspires to be?"

"An actor," Halston replied.

"All actors have a day job," I argued.

Halston began, "His day job is to-"

"Fuck you?" Giuseppe yelled at him.

It became apparent that Halston was embarrassed by the outburst and quickly hushed Giuseppe, begging him not to cause a scene in front of a guest. But he could not be calmed. In the short time the pair had known each other, a matter of weeks, Giuseppe had become oppressed within the confines of Halston's wanton propriety. He did not know whether he was the wife or the mistress, the slave or the servant. This was not because Halston was unclear to Giuseppe but because Halston was unclear to himself. For Halston, Giuseppe was a beautiful, lavish toy, just as the New Florentine yacht was. Had Halston not been rich and made in to a moderately handsome man by his dermatologist, he would have been completely undeserving of such a thing. It had been the lure of Halston's career and lifestyle that kept Giuseppe with him, not his personality or candor. For Giuseppe to proclaim his independence in writing a novel, Halston's importance was threatened. No longer would Giuseppe need Halston for survival. Giuseppe could soon have a life as similarly sumptuous to Halston's if the book was received admiringly by the public. This duality was best illustrated seven minutes in to the feud when Halston shouted, "I don't want a fuck-buddy, I want a friend!" Sans any poetry, the statement was able to convince Giuseppe of Halston's amorous intentions. It displayed Halston's sympathy for Giuseppe's need to be more than just a kept boy. It was Halston saying, "You matter to me." When they dismissed themselves with the excuse of "going to look at Giuseppe's manuscript," I imagined it was Halston's way of summoning Giuseppe to the bedroom.

ATROCITIES OF THE BOUDOIR

Bryan Madden ambushed me. It was just after I got off the phone with my publisher, having raved to him about *Ecstasy* and its author Giuseppe Tavolo, that I found him standing at the open door of my bedroom. He had no words for me at first and I had none for him but felt obligated to say something. It's not every day another man suddenly kisses you without warning or context.

"How's Olive?" I blurted. "I haven't seen her much."

"She's good. Working on her book."

"I thought she wasn't writing."

"It's not a novel, it's a textbook," he said, his smile gleaming with a shield of white teeth.

"She's going in to teaching?"

"I don't know... the book's called *Songs To Get Raped To*." As he said this we simultaneously found how ridiculous the title was and shared a precarious laugh. It was just what the cumbersome moment needed. This led Bryan to enter the bedroom and sit down on the sofa across from me at the desk.

"What are you writing?" he asked.

"What does it matter?" I said, immediately annoyed at his second attempt to uncover my project still in production.

"I'm sorry. I'm just trying to be friendly." He lowered his voice. "I feel like a jerk for kissing you. But I just can't keep it back."

"What? That you're a gay?"

"I'm not gay. I just feel something for you."

"How can you say that? If you're gay, you're gay, if you're not you're not." When I heard myself say these things I went over and closed the door to the bedroom. For someone to overhear our conversation could have easily bankrupted both our reputations.

"You're not the first guy I've been attracted to, but I've never acted on it before because it wasn't worth it. To throw my marriage away on something so meaningless? I'd be a fool." Bryan was now at the point of shame, condemning his own impulses. Even if I didn't agree with his actions I wasn't going to let him mutilate his own esteem.

"It's not worthless." I said, "If you're having homosexual feelings it's a completely valid desire to act on them."

"Haven't you ever been attracted to a guy? I often think that most men are bisexual but they suppress it."

"No," I said, then thought back to all the men I'd known as friends, recalling my best friend in high school. His name was Gregg. We'd spent every moment together for years and one summer I don't think we were apart for more than maybe the duration of a bathroom break. But then Gregg met Jennifer, his first serious girlfriend. Gregg began spending all his time with her, making me feel not only abandoned but betrayed, as though he'd cheated on me. As a way of easing tensions, I told Bryan the story of Gregg and how at the time I discarded my emotions as feelings of neglect or jealousy but now came to realize my feelings for him had been more than platonic, that at various times I wanted to hug Gregg or touch him but wouldn't because of social standings, thinking straight men don't do that.

"It's not that black and white," Bryan said. "I wish it were."

"You're bisexual?" I asked.

"Yes."

"And sick of pussy?" He laughed at my vulgarity.

"Not exactly. I've just come to realize the beauty of a man."

"In me?"

"Yes."

"When did you realize that you liked me?" I asked.

He was about to speak, then hesitated, smiled, and asked, "You really want to know?"

"Absolutely," I prompted. "We're adults, I can handle anything you tell me."

"Years ago when you wrote your first book. You were on one of those morning television shows promoting it. The newscast made your book sound really interesting, and the interview made you look so, I don't know – alluring. You were wearing this really great suit with no tie. I remember wanting to go out and buy the same exact thing. At the same time I bought the suit I also bought a copy of your book. I read the whole thing in about two days... which is really quick for me because I don't read a lot. I'm used to 90-page scripts, not 400-page novels. Anyway, I recommended the book to a friend, they read it, liked it, and said I should consider optioning it from you. At once I was giddy, thinking if I did that I'd be able to meet you in person. It was crazy because your book is so erratic, so fluid in its own consciousness."

"It's a book about nothing," I said.

"It really is! But it's also about *everything*. I knew then it'd make a horrible movie, which honestly it did," we both laughed at the inference, "but I still had to buy it. And so I called my agent and she called yours and I impatiently waited for the day we met in New York. I wore my new suit to our meeting and new shoes and cologne and got my haircut special. It wasn't until I shook your hand and felt my cock harden I realized I wanted you in a sexual way. Prior to that I thought I just idolized you. Like people do for their favorite musician or sports star. When my hand touched yours I felt a sensation I only had a few other times in my life. It was a kind of electric shock of the nerves. Before then I'd never considered touching a man. But after that encounter I couldn't think of anything I wanted to do more than experience a man."

"Damn," I exclaimed. He wasn't keeping anything back.

"And I wanted to impress you that day so I offered you as much as I could afford for the rights. Of course you accepted the deal and I invited you out for a drink."

"You did?" I asked.

"Yes."

"I don't remember going out for a drink."

"We didn't. You said you were flying back to Seattle that day."

"That's right."

"You broke my heart, yet I didn't even fully realize it in the moment. Even when I had a raging hard on during the meeting sex never crossed my mind. My only thought was that I wanted to be your friend. I wanted to get to know you better. I thought if I turned your book in to a movie you'd be one of those authors who has to have a say about every camera angle, the lighting, the music – *all of it!* I was hoping you'd be on set every single day for months. The idea of you being in my life every day became so appealing I was ready to do anything I could to make it happen."

"How could you not realize what you were feeling?"

"I don't know," he said in exasperation. "My psychiatrist tells me to do what I feel I should do. But she knows I'm such a coward that I won't do it so all the inner turmoil I create causes me to visit her more often. She's one brilliant lady."

"If you liked me, why did you treat me like garbage during production of the movie?" I asked.

"Between the time of our first meeting and production began on the film, what, seven months? Over that time I began to realize what my fascination for you meant and began to reject the idea, which was probably my own homophobia kicking in. I loathed you but still wanted you. I hated that you had such a power over me. It was so ironic… I'd made you a multi-millionaire and you blew me off – so to speak. But then you met my wife."

"And she cheated on you with me." I said, "That must have been humiliating."

"Actually, it renewed my fascination of you. When she came home after fucking you at the Hotel Bel-Air I'd make love to her and get off knowing that when I tasted her, literally moments after you'd finished fucking her, I could taste what remained of you in her."

Bryan was perverted and aloof. Never had I had sex with Olive at the Hotel Bel-Air or anywhere in Los Angeles, merely on the yacht in years past. I did not tell Bryan this but explained how interested I was in his sexual discovery while thinking of how he found gratification in touching the woman who'd just been touched by another man. Bryan was receiving pleasure by imagining a man touching what belonged to him. It was sexual stimulation by proxy.

"Have you ever had sex with a man?" I queried. It was a question that would have been better unasked.

"No. Honestly, I wouldn't know where to begin," Bryan blushed.

EXPECTATIONS

After Monday night's dinner I skipped a film screening presented by Bryan Madden. The yet to be released film, titled *Hollywood Boulevard*, was purported to be Bryan Madden's most creatively involved picture, chronicling the rise and fall of a winsome starlet too fragile to endure the compulsive brutality of the Hollywood mass-media publicity machine and global fame. It was an art house pleaser meant as a tribute to the films of late 1930s and early 1940s.

It had not been my intention to avoid the others once again, but became unexpectedly confounded over the piece of writing I was working on. *The Fetus's Tale* had no meaning, no message, no heart or soul. It was exposition for the sake of shock, and I began to dislike it. The story was entertainment, nothing more than the tickling of taboos, and so I shredded the pieces I'd printed and tossed them out the window in to the sea. I deleted the file and placed Katrin's computer back in her bedroom with a note that read: "Thanks, but no thanks." In doing this the burden of finishing a piece of writing I was not altogether passionate about evaporated and I was free to think up a new story, or not. Doing nothing was my new forte. I was now determined to merely observe but not initiate an editorial. As Bryan Madden said, my first book, along with its successors, were about nothing more than simple, random observations in a stranger's life. They were not poetic or philosophical but plain descriptive surveillance of what at first glance appears as commonplace things but upon further examination are nothing less than extraordinary. I was not creating worlds inside my novels but recreating in prose the world I was actually living within. The definition of an artist is one who creates and I had ceased in doing so. My signature, so-called gift to literature was my ability to highlight absurdities in everyday reality we'd all become accustom to. Sure there were some absurdities on the ship I could study.

After the movie party Katrin came in to my room.

"Packing so soon? There's still tomorrow," she said.

"I'm just eager to get to San Francisco," I said as I zipped up my duffle bag.

"So you can immediately fly home?" she asked drolly.

"Yes." It disappointed me to find that other people knew me so well. I tried so hard to be unpredictable and enigmatic. How had everyone figured me out?

She sat down at the desk and noticed her computer was gone.

"I put the computer in your room," I said.

"Did you finish it?" she asked with eagerness.

"No. It wasn't going anywhere."

"Maybe it just needs to ferment," she encouraged. "Give it some time."

"It's fermenting in the Pacific."

"What?"

"I tore it up and threw it out the goddamn window."

"What the hell for?" she erupted. "It was brilliant!"

"It was contrite and pretentious," I countered. My true belief was the story had become too self-observant and tongue-in-cheek to be considered a serious work depicting precognitive emotion. There were other aspects of the story which hindered its ability to be forthright, such as the possibility for readers to interpret it as anti-abortion literature. I learned early on in my writing career to steer clear of political dust ups with readers. Never in the modern history of publishing has an author benefitted him or herself by alienating half their readership, as making any stance on abortion was likely to do. My original aim with the story had been to examine how a grown man or woman could enter the figurative womb of the psyche in order to examine the origins of one's mind. If this person scrutinized their earliest sensations, devastations and triumphs it could illuminate why their mind desires and detests what it does.

"If you don't examine your mistakes how are you supposed to ever learn from them?" Katrin ridiculed just as she exited the room. I followed her down the hallway and in to her room.

"What's the matter?" I asked. Wanting to get laid I had no intention of upsetting Katrin. "It was just a story," I pleaded, resulting in her slamming the bedroom door shut. Slowly I opened the door and calmly walked in, shutting the door behind me. This was the first time I noticed there were no locks on any of the doors on the ship, not even the bathrooms.

"Are you ever going to move on?" Katrin asked, her inclination unclear to me.

"Move on from what?"

"This phase you're in of endless brooding mixed with fits of meaningless contemplation," she lambasted. "Everyone is sick of it. It got old five years ago."

"Nobody's said anything."

"Because they're your friends!"

"Isn't a friend supposed to tell a person the truth no matter how hurtful? Is that not the measure of a true friend?"

"Excuse me, they're being *friendly*. No one on this boat is a true friend. We all have agendas here."

"What's yours?"

"To show my father I'm legitimate and that other writers value what I do and that I'm not just a provocateur. I want him to see my work impacting the lives of the women who read it. Women talk to each other differently because of my writing. They're more open and living more honestly. Not many writers can claim that."

"If you wanted to accomplish that you should've taken him to a book signing in Manhattan. You're a goddess to women there. But here you're nothing more than a pop-lit scribe. No one here respects you."

"You're only saying that because I've out-sold and out-fucked you. Any author, no matter how lauded, suddenly becomes garbage to you people once they hit the bestsellers list. All of you on this ship hate each other with such a passion but interact as if you're all friends. It sickens me. It's more sinister than anything any of us has written about. Even that pig Halston with his police precinct orgy novellas."

Katrin had riddled me with such a furor I then grasped she really was the hardened, self-sufficient female hybrid she depicted in her string of biographical urban anecdotes.

"*Out-fucked me?*" I said back with just enough smarminess to make her rethink her rage. Quoting Katrin was always a great way to mirror back her own ridiculousness.

"Yes, out-fucked." She elaborated, "I'm a bigger whore than you are and you're jealous."

"No, I'm not jealous. I've always known you were a bigger whore than me. It would take decades for me to catch up to you." My comment meant no harm and was truthful in every detail but Katrin was not humored. She dismissed me from her room and I quietly conceded defeat. I'd pissed her off just as I was always pissing the women in my life off. Maybe women, in general, are just too responsive. Sometimes I think they're more competitive than men, especially when it's woman versus woman. Modern sisterhood is dead. It's every bitch for herself nowadays, and perhaps it's always been this way.

Somewhere during the day I'd promised my body it was going to be having sex with Katrin later that night. When I wound up alone in my bed, trying desperately to fall asleep and to end another miserable day on the yacht, any random thought about any vaguely attractive woman was able to provoke my manhood. Recalling Katrin's bedroom antics, of how well equipped and trained she was in pleasing men - how I'd came so fast and so many times with her that all the sex was now strung in to one long anthology of fulfillment – caused me to immediately begin stroking myself. But the night was too hot to remain under the covers and so I flung them on the floor. In the dim fraction of light I peered down at my erection and at both my eager hands massaging it intermittently with dawdling, prolonged strokes to prevent eruption. Not a minute in to pleasing myself I could already feel the hot fluid inside me ready to flutter out on to the bed.

I closed my eyes and imagined Katrin sitting on it, moaning with the same ferocity she debated me with and bouncing up and down on me, often in a way that hurt my legs but I allowed her to do so because she was so engulfed with pleasure by it. The only thing she seemed to enjoy more was when I devoured her sweltering pink slit. For her to see me down there, knowing I could be tamed, manipulated, conquered and spent, so defiled and my face grotesquely absorbed with her orifice, must have thrilled her immensely.

The fondling slowed as I felt I could come with just one strong tug. I wanted to prolong my orgasm as long as possible while recalling everything Katrin and I had done together. But even when I completely stopped and took my hands away the sensation didn't stop. I opened my eyes and looked down again to see Bryan at the foot of my bed. He was in his pajamas, smiling, with one tender hand on my erection. He stroked me even slower than I did myself. When our eyes met and I failed to react with rage he took this as consent to go further. Silently he knelt down and placed me in his mouth, caressing it with his tongue like no woman had ever done before. Being a man, he knew precisely how to stimulate another man and to watch for the testicles to contract closer to the body when near ejaculation, at which time he'd decelerate his pace. The sensations shooting through my body felt so overwhelming I don't think I could have stopped Bryan. The bliss overtook me, so much so that when I did finally discharge my spine began to arc, as if I were doing a sit-up. As the fervent pulsating of my climax receded I could feel my heart hammering inside my chest. It was unclear to me if this marathon of palpitations was from the exertion of my orgasm or the adrenaline spawned from doing something so daring and spontaneous as letting another man suck me off.

When he was finished Bryan did not smile or display any indication of delight. Before I was able to contemplate what kind of retribution he might request I perform on him he left the room, saying nothing. I quickly wiped the fluid off my chest and stomach with a T-shirt and covered myself with the bed sheets again. I quickly dozed off, neither contemplating my sexuality or the effect this little incident might have on other's we were involved with.

OUTINGS

When a single black balloon drifted ominously down from the blue sky, mingled briefly with the surface of the platinum sea and then jumped up on to the deck of the New Florentine, I knew we were approaching the Bay Area. This unforeseen stranger was very much welcome for it signaled an end to this queer journey of corrupt intellects who'd soon return to their fragmented and embellished lives within the societies which adored them.

"Where in the world did you get that?" Olive Snow asked me as I brought the balloon in to the ship's main dining room. A buffet of fruits and pastries was being gobbled up by everyone around me, none of whom believed me when I explained the origins of the lone balloon. It was the first time every guest had assembled together in one room since the first day.

"We're a half mile from the shore," Halston chuckled, "what are the odds of finding a balloon!"

"One in a trillion?"

"At least!" Giuseppe jollily concluded. He was in his finest mood yet having that same morning come out of the closet as an author. The previous evening he'd let Tom Reynolds have a look through his material. Like me, Tom found the manuscript to be witty and dangerously entertaining – like nothing written in the last two decades. It was radical and completely counter-culture. Now everyone demanded to see the book, currently being scurried through by Katrin as she ate a pile of melon balls. As she quickly read through the pages she would erupt with laughter or amused contempt at all the outrageous moments the novel was peppered with. Never before had I witnessed a novel being dissecting within the atmosphere of a party. To be passed around like an intoxicating joint or exotic curio was the highest compliment a book could be paid because it meant it was able to encroach on the imagination of everyone who held it. Few novels can accomplish such a feat.

"What is a writer's worth anymore?" William Zofield asked of the group. It was his belief that with the emergence of the Internet we now found ourselves in a global village where mass communication is neglected and overused, the novelist is no more unique than any man or woman text messaging their friend, spouse, or parent. More so, everyone was documenting their lives with the permanence of the digital medium. Whether they realized it or not, people were going to be remembered by their Facebook and Twitter posts. No longer was a novel a forum of personal introspection or societal examination, but a means to push products. Blogs are immediate, relevant in the moment, but also abundant and tremendously perishable. Popular authors (nameless ones of course) were now openly discussing how they'd written in to their stories the names of specific products (e.g. Mercedes-Benz, Rolex, Four Seasons hotels) because they were offered cash by said companies to do so. The practice of product placement was rampant in Hollywood films but deemed unethical by many in the New York publishing indusrty. That was until those houses were gobbled up in to the massive corporate circuses that sold everything from booze and shotguns to hotel room porn and literature! Suddenly America's finest wits were writing of gloriously beautiful and ethical characters talking on their fashionable Apple iPhones while flying around the globe exclusively on British Airways.

"I've accepted product placement cash," admitted Halston.

"From who?" Olive asked.

"Remember that scene in my novel, *Gringo Lingo*, where Drake confronts Fabian about his illicit desire?" A thousand disjointed glances were shot across the room.

"Yeah, what about it?" I could tell from her response she had never read *Gringo Lingo*.

"I so delicately mentioned the name of the lube the boys slather themselves in before doing it bareback."

"Cancun Lubricants Incorporated? That's a real company?" Tom Reynolds ragged, "I thought you made that name up, it sounds ridiculous." I was astounded to hear Tom Reynolds, a retired Navy man and father of five, knew the brand name of the lube used in one of Halston's books. Such precise details, known off the cuff, were usually known only by the authors of such work and their endearing super fans.

"Nope." Halston responded, "They're *huge*. They have something like a seventeen percent market share of the gay men's lubricant industry."

"That really is huge," Tom agreed.

"How much did they pay you?" quizzed William.

"Five hundred dollars," admitted Halston.

"Advertising comes cheap," William replied.

Halston added "...a week for the rest of my life."

"It's a lube pension!" I commented.

"I've made over twenty-thousand off it so far. Sadly, that's more than the royalties on the hardback edition."

"Everybody's gotta make a buck," Tom Reynolds noted. He knew a thing or two about making money from side projects related to publishing.

"Enough about money," Halston droned, "let's chat about what inspires us. I'm sure we all have very interesting muses and sources of encouragement. After all, that is why we are here, to help each other."

"Then you first Mr. Levy," I politely required.

"Alright," he agreed, "I find harmony in the arts, particularly with the ballet or opera, but most of my encouragement comes from youth."

"Teenage wildlife?" Katrin jeered with insinuation.

"No. Youth culture. The era of naivety we all experienced late in our teens and in to our twenties when everything seemed possible and the ambition to succeed was rampant and widespread."

"As was chlamydia," Olive ridiculed.

"Enough!" I demanded, "We're not here to judge or out-wit each other. This is not a competition."

"What's your inspiration Marc?" Olive asked. "Or is it possible you haven't found it yet because your creativity has been parched for a while now?"

"It's not parched," Katrin defended me. "He's just a purger."

"I thought anorexics were waifish," Bryan said. "Marc is downright strapping." His comment could have been deemed a testimonial of sexual appeal but the others were, at that point anyway, completely unaware of Bryan and my peculiar encounters and the compliment was overlooked at once.

"He doesn't have an eating disorder," Katrin clarified, "It's a writing disorder. He is so concerned with the quality of his work and has such tantrums when anyone analyzes it that instead of revising and rewriting it he throws the whole thing out, never to recreate the world he's formed."

"I used to do that," Tom divulged. "Just after college I tried to write the great American novel. After I finished it I thought it to be crap and threw it in the recycle bin. That same day a lady who was living in the same apartment house went to throw out some newspapers and found the book and read it. She thought the book was magnificent and tracked me down to tell me how much she liked it. I thanked her but explained that it was far from my best work, despite it being my only work at the time. She became appalled when I told her the copy she'd read was the only copy, that it was not some draft or spare. Long story short… she became my agent, and found me a publisher in New York in less than a month. That book was a rather decent seller."

"Cheers to nosy neighbors!" I hailed.

"If she was smart she would have erased your name and published it under her own name," Olive suggested.

"She was probably one of those identity thieves!" William said. "Unable to find credit card receipts or bank statements she settled for a thousand pages on why the rich are getting richer and the poor are getting diabetes."

"You've read my first book!" Tom rejoiced. To have been read by William Zofield was a prestigious honor for any author.

"No, I saw the movie," said William.

"Which version?" Tom asked.

"There's more than one?" inquired Giuseppe.

"The British television version," William sated.

"Is that the one with the actress from *Absolutely Fabulous*?" I asked.

"No," Katrin said, "you're thinking of *French and Saunders*."

"It's the same woman," determined William.

"I'm sorry but I haven't watched the BBC since I was a fetus," Katrin declared.

"Inspiration people!" reminded Halston. "We're talking about inspiration, not little old ladies who sift through the trash looking for things to read or what's playing on the tele in England."

"Fringe theater gets me off," Olive broadcast. "I love works in progress and knowing the performance I'm seeing is not a thoroughly mechanized and refined version but one of spontaneity and experimentation – it gives me the chills."

I turned to Olive to ask her if she'd seen any shows in Seattle. In recent years Seattle had become a scorching hot bed of experimental live theater. There didn't seem to be a basement or attic that hadn't hosted a production of some sort. The whole movement, meant to be the antithesis of Broadway style productions, was beginning to define the Pacific Northwest arts scene.

"I arrived a week before we were to set sail. I think I saw eight shows. There's nothing like having to walk down some grimy back alley, down a set of creaky old stairs, and in to a musty old grand dame of a playhouse, to see a play more real than life itself. It was truly enchanting." This remark was the first friendly accordance we shared since she'd broken off our affair. To be at peace with Olive, a volatile poet known for her tinges of dangerous philosophy, came as a wash of relief and safety. If I had to decide who on the ship was most likely to whip out a pistol and shoot someone in the skull it would have been Olive Snow.

"What inspires the purger?" asked Tom, referring to me. The Purger was at once my crude new moniker.

"The countryside," I said, "self-sufficiency, solace, the catharsis of nature."

"I hate nature," Katrin riled me. "It's cruel and unjust. Life is not valued, only survival and reproduction."

"As a New Yorker," I addressed Katrin, "you are thoroughly aware of what is cruel and unjust. You live in a city of paradoxes where people pay fifteen dollars to sleep for twenty minutes in a mechanism known as a napping pod but repeal ordinances that enable the homeless to bathe and defecate indoors."

"What is it about you and New York?" Katrin raised, "You're bitter!"

"And as for reproduction," I continued, "you celebrate the fact you spend many nights in the act of procreation, absorbing every bit of gratification while preventing the consequence."

"So what!" she rebelled.

Halston began clanging his melon stabber on his mimosa glass to declare once more, "Inspiration! Let's just talk about inspiration god damn it!"

"Fuck inspiration!" William boomed. "Let's discuss what ails us and what distracts and torments us!"

"What diverts you father?" Katrin asked him.

"Television. Mother-fucking-reality-television!"

We all laughed at his confession, thinking it to be a gag, but when he started in on all the docu-dramas he'd recently found himself attached to and was currently in withdrawal from having been on the ship for days, the concept that a generation's greatest writer might be corrupted by something as cheap and insignificant as exploitive reality television became appalling and sad. It was almost a warning to all of us on the dangers of popular culture.

"If I had to pick one thing," Tom said, "my biggest distraction would be my wife. She's always trying to accommodate me and make sure I have everything I need to do my work. But it seems she does more harm than good. She's an absolute fuss. But don't any of you tell her that because it would completely destroy her."

"My ailment is men," Katrin admitted.

"Me too," Halston avowed.

"I thought it was models," I said.

"If presented the opportunity I might screw a fashion model," he replied.

"No, those model cars." I sighed.

"Those cars are therapy, not a distraction."

"My guilty pleasure is sex," Olive feted without shame. "If my husband was ever home I wouldn't ever write. We'd just fuck all day."

"Don't I know it!" Bryan recalled, "When the studio shutdown last fall because of the actor's strike I took Olive to Venice for our anniversary. I'll just say we saw very little of the Grand Canal but every inch of that hotel room."

"What's your biggest distraction from writing Giuseppe?" I asked, intending to include the new writer.

"Nothing distracts me. It is the only thing I can't be distracted from. Everything I do is distracted by my writing. I am always building stories in my brain no matter what I am doing. I can be folding laundry, making love, or swimming in the ocean, and never do I stop thinking about the story I'm working on." Giuseppe's answer was a glaring testament to his credentials as a true, honest-to-god writer. It caused a shallow lull in the conversation.

"Life distracts me endlessly," I said, to which I received a multitude of questioning and despondent glances. "Just observing everything, you know, the way things move and smell and react to other variables. We live in such a diverse environment. There's too much to experience."

"One thing! Name one fucking thing!" Olive blasted. I could tell the group loved her aggression as they all smiled and smirked upon her eruption.

"Outside my office window there's this tree where a squirrel lives. Whenever I sit down to write something he'll always start doing something like collecting food or attacking birds. He's the biggest nuisance and I absolutely despise him because he always steals my concentration."

"Is the squirrel's name Grayson?" Ashley asked.

"Yes, how did you know that?" I said.

"Because you wrote about him in your second book," she replied. "He ended up burning down the professor's house."

Just then Halston invited everyone to shoot clay pigeons off the back of the boat but I declined, as did William Zofield who asked to speak with me alone. As the others jollily marched off to gun down flying discs I sat next to William at the table as he read through Giuseppe's manuscript.

"How can I help you?" I said.

"It's about my daughter," he quietly replied. "I've been told you're involved with her."

"If by involved you mean dating, we're just-" I stammered as I searched for the right word.

"Fucking?" he interjected curtly. Between statements he would read lines from Giuseppe's book. I'd never seen someone so engrossed in a novel that they couldn't put it aside while talking to someone. William was so enrapt he paused sporadically to read the next sentence. Giuseppe's book was that good.

"That pretty much sums it up," I said. "Except I think she's done with that. And with me entirely."

"You broke up?"

"We were never together. We merely stopped having casual sex," I said. William let out a beleaguered chuckle, the source of which must have been the manuscript in front of him as he failed to take his eyes off the page.

"Did she say why?" he asked a moment later.

"No. She doesn't talk a lot."

"She's always lived by the motto of 'actions speak louder than words.'"

"I realize that," I said with a tone of annoyance. I was a bit disturbed by William reading and talking at the same time. It was as rude as someone talking on their telephone in a library. When I stopped talking he put his thumb in the book and closed it.

"She didn't tell you she saw you kissing Bryan on the beach?" William said this as if it were nothing, like someone revealing they'd witnessed someone picking strawberries or riding a bike.

He was so casual and I was embarrassed that he knew of the event. I couldn't think of a response but couldn't allow myself to lie to him. I wouldn't let ego or vanity lower myself to that. And so I shrugged and pretended it really was nothing.

"It didn't mean anything," I said palely.

"Maybe not to you or even Bryan. But it did to her. She doesn't need to pick up the pieces of another broken heart. Katrin has too hard of a time opening up to people as it is. The genre of literature she's cultivated is a veil to hide human vulnerability and a disproportionate fear of rejection."

"Listen William," I stated boldly, "he's the one who kissed me. I was shocked that he did it and wish he hadn't. I'm sorry she saw it and I'll talk to her about it. But let's get something straight, we were never involved emotionally with each other, only physically."

"Marc," he patronized, "she may pretend to consume and dispose of all the men she romances, but I know that she is just waiting until one of her lovers turns to her and offers her a relationship. Then she will concede and fall in love."

"How do you know that?"

"I'm her father. Despite what she says we keep in touch. I read her books and the articles she writes. You can learn more about a person reading the fiction they write than the nonfiction."

"You really think so?"

"I know so." With this William picked up his glass of orange juice, surely diluted with vodka, and walked out on the boat's deck to shoot discs with the others. I knew him then to be a fool, unaware there actually were such things as feeble, manipulative sluts and that he'd never considered his daughter to be one. A real woman, one of resilience and fortitude, would not have hesitated to call the man she was seeing or sleeping with on his absurd actions, no matter how she perceived them.

THE PERFECT MARRIAGE

"Since when are you bisexual?" Ashley whispered in my ear as we both sat in view of Olive Snow aiming a rifle in to the sky and whining of how heavy the gun was.

"I'm not," I replied smoothly.

"I interviewed Bryan Madden for the book and he says you and him fooled around last night. Can you believe he'd say something like that?"

"We did," I acknowledged, privately outraged he'd be so open about his newfound sexual cravings. This sent Ashley in to an insane fit of hilarity she tried to muzzle with her palm.

"What the fuck? What are you up to?" she begged for more information.

"He's been flirting with me for days now. Last night he snuck in to my room and took things in to his own hands... and mouth."

We were both now cackling wildly in our sun chairs like teens still discovering all the components of sex and desire. This was followed by a multitude of perturbed glances from the competing marksmen who were rather distraught that we found their shooting skills to be so hilarious.

As is archetypical Ashley, her mood turned from merry to morose within a moment.

"Something horrific and terrible is going on," she cried.

"What's worse than getting an unwanted blowjob from the husband of your ex-mistress?"

"I'm sleeping with Tom Reynolds."

"Tom is married," I blasted as loudly as one could without being heard by others not five yards away. If her revelation was true and Ashley had been capable of corroding the vows of Tom and his wife Susan, it would be the fourth marriage she'd be credited with destroying.

"They've been separated for three months," she discreetly explained. "He's going to divorce her." Just as she uttered this Tom's turn to shoot clay pigeons came up. As he loaded the rifle he waved a hand at Ashley and smiled. He surely wanted to impress her.

"What about the guy?" I asked.

"What guy?"

"The philanthropist who flew up to Seattle with you. Isn't he waiting to pick you up at the pier?" I asked.

"There is no philanthropist," she crumbled. "I moved to San Francisco to start a new life and I'm still waiting for it to begin. If I told you it had been years since I had a relationship it would sound pathetic, wouldn't it?"

"No, it wouldn't," I replied.

"Maybe not to you, you're used to being alone. But for someone to spend a whole year in a new city of new people and not once find a mate, it's not just pathetic, it's catastrophic."

"You're so over dramatic. I love you."

We watched as Tom fired in to the air, hitting all the discs. He received a brief interlude of applause from the other novices. Merrily he walked over to Ashley and sat down next to her as she pretended to be so daunted by his skill. They did not hold hands or show affection in front of the others. Surely they'd let their fondness build and swell until they were alone. In contrast to Tom and Ashley's stealth, Olive and Bryan's affections were open for everyone to see. They held hands, kissed each other nonchalantly every so couple of minutes and were never seen more than a few feet apart at all times. I understood their public fondling to be all a show, displaying the entire extent of their physical relationship for all to view. They looked married and happy so most everyone who didn't know them concluded they were.

I have always found those people banal enough to complain about the weather to be life's most tedious breed. When it was noticed by the group that a great number of steely, bulbous clouds were rolling in towards San Francisco Bay to the south of us, an argument of whether or not this weather would cause thunder and lightning broke out. It was Tom's opinion (being a mid-westerner made him an expert in judging a cloud's significance) that the clouds would be undisruptive, using the tired analogy of "all bark and no bite" to proclaim the cumuli's supposed harmlessness. But Olive wouldn't hear it. She touted the cloud's unique coastal Californian formation, thus making them a different, more volatile creed than the clouds Tom knew. Then Giuseppe shared his experience with Mediterranean clouds, William explained the mystery of English Channel clouds, and finally Halston started in on his experiences with Gulf of Mexico clouds. During this Bryan was able to elude all suspicions and take a seat next to me.

"I can't do this anymore," Bryan said to me within ear shot of Ashley who was documenting the milieu of lunacy on her computer.

"Can't do what anymore?" I asked.

"Anything and everything," he sulked. "I don't want to go back to Hollywood. I hate it there."

"You hate your job?" I asked, already knowing the answer. If there was one thing I knew Bryan didn't hate it was producing films.

"No, I love my job more than anything. I would never walk away from the studio. I just despise what I've become."

"What have you become?" I prodded.

"A complete lie," he replied glumly, deflating back in to the deck chair.

"Then what's keeping you from telling the truth?"

"It'd be too disastrous, too sinister. I've let this all happen. It could all look to premeditated."

"Are you sure?" I rose, "you definitely wouldn't be the first player in Hollywood to shed the protection of the closet."

"I know. Maybe that's why. It wouldn't be original."

"But it would be truthful. Truth is the origin of originality."

Bryan layed down on the reclining chair next to me as Olive came over to see what it was we were talking about. I think she was the only person on the boat who didn't know about me and Bryan.

"It's your turn to shoot Marc," she said, a sure attempt to pry me from the presence of her husband. She'd very likely become apprehensive as to why he always hovered near me. It must have drove her crazy to see her husband consumed by the attention of the same lover she rejected.

"I don't play with guns," I declined. "They're dangerous, especially around people who don't know what they're doing with them, not to mention perpetually intoxicated."

"It's a twenty-two. You couldn't blow your head off with it if you tried," she said. Ashley became raucous as she realized the double entendre.

"If only you knew honey!" Ashley said to herself and Tom. He was in on the joke.

"Fine, I'll take your turn," Olive said.

"Why'd you marry such a bitch?" I asked Bryan after she left to go shoot more discs.

"I was too busy to notice," Bryan replied. "And when I did notice it was too late to do anything about it."

"There's always divorce," I proposed.

"But I love her too much. She's my best friend."

"Then you really are fucked."

Ashley, who'd been conversing with Tom about a secret holiday rendezvous in Chicago sometime around Thanksgiving, turned to Bryan and asked, "What have you boys been up to?"

"Does it matter?" Bryan glowered.

"I just want to get the details right for the book," she explained with a dour shrug.

"Ashley, what's my name in your book?" I asked, assuming she'd have the decency to fictionalize the outing.

"It's Marc Mulberry."

"How dare you," I huffed, "can't it be something glamorous? Maybe Jean-Luc Balzac de Loire?"

"No. The story would lose its credibility if I were to strip you of your identities."

"Damn you."

"What exactly is the book about?" Tom asked her. "It's not a diary is it?"

"It's a memoir of sorts," she answered. "A chronicle of peculiar observations."

"Could I convince you to omit something?" I asked directly.

"What?" Tom interfered.

"Oh, it's nothing." I reddened. Tom, the man-of-men, the ghost of Hemingway, the most masculine guy I knew and most stubborn of the whole bunch, despite his outright friendly nature, was the last person I wanted to know of my tryst with Bryan. If anything, Tom was the man I wanted to be. He was the epitome of man every boy attempts to live up to. He was larger than life. An avid fishermen, amateur carpenter, Gulf War vet, frequent kayaker, and a baseball player. Surely he'd keep me at a further, more disgusted distance if he knew I'd been sucked off by another man.

"Are you talking about the blowjob?" Tom asked, shushed so the others still shooting at discs would not hear.

"Yes he is," Ashley confirmed.

"How do you know about that?" I asked, cupping my forehead in my hands in embarrassment.

"It was the blowjob heard 'round the world," Tom joked. He and everyone else were fairly well socially lubricated by the breakfast libations. I figured if he were sober his reaction would have been a little less rollicking.

"Can't we talk about something else? This is humiliating," I said.

"What's with the weather?" Ashley moaned.

Tom stood up from his seat next to Ashley and sat down right next to me, patting his hand on my knee very casually. Whispering, he said in my ear, "It's no big deal. The sea will do that to a man. I spent eight years in the Navy. I know how it can be when you're feeling lonely, you've spent weeks at sea, you haven't touched a woman in just as long and suddenly you brush up against another sailor and you have this overwhelming sensation of affection."

"You can't be serious," I muttered. For Tom to blame the grimacing sea for turning my sexuality in to something of ambivalence was at the least absurd.

"All I'm saying is we're all human. We've all done things we wish we hadn't, but life goes on. Any drunk will tell you that." Just as Tom said this the four of us turned to witness William Zofield swinging his rifle wildly at the water trying to shoot a shark he claimed to have seen splash up against the ship.

"What if he enjoyed it immensely?" Bryan quizzed.

"Of course he enjoyed it, that's not the point," Tom replied. "Physical pleasure is pleasure no matter who is administering it. A goat could have given him head and he would have enjoyed it. The source of pleasure is irrelevant."

"I'm not sure that's the case," I replied.

"How can you continue to lie to her?" Ashley summoned of Bryan. "You two appear to be the perfect Hollywood husband and wife."

"That's a contradiction," he replied. "There is no perfect Hollywood husband and wife."

"What about Goldie and Kurt?" Tom asserted.

"Just like Hollywood, our marriage is an intricate production of scripted and rehearsed moments. When we're not in front of the camera, so to speak, she has her lovers and I have mine."

"You should write a book," Tom suggested.

"Yes!" Ashley agreed, then added the title, "*The Double Life & Times of Bryan Madden.*"

"I *am* writing a book," Bryan said. "It's fiction though."

"Fiction is for faggots," Ashley derided. "Write something highly autobiographical. But change the names around and add some extra drama, like a gunfight or car chase at the end. When the book comes out it will be regarded as fiction but in forty years when we're all dead and pop culture historians look back on you, your career and life, they'll consider your book to be the most accurate of biographies. It will be glamorous."

"Sounds like *A Moveable Feast*," said Tom.

"Yes, but Bryan's not a pathological liar like Hemingway," Ashley rebuffed.

This last comment was the baiting to a trademark Ashley Mulberry trap. She, as well as anyone, knew I was a complete and utter Ernest Hemingway fanatic. He is and was a legend for so many reasons; his tragedy, his determination, and maybe a little for his machismo. He was the biggest character anyone could ever think up. He is missed so terribly by so many people. They don't make novelists like him anymore. For Ashley to so easily debase the man – an inspiration to so many contemporary writers who knew anything about him – demonstrated to everyone within earshot she would never be and could never be a true writer.

When the firing squad ceased, Tom and Ashley rejoined the others in order to lounge around, lazily, as we'd all done for most of the trip already. Together they would arrange an impromptu ski trip to Lake Tahoe via San Francisco upon docking. Of course Olive fettered the idea, proclaiming her fear of mountain passes; William mentioned a story he'd seen on TV stating how polluted the lake and air around it had become; and Halston, never to be out-hosted took offense that someone would dare utilize the commencement of this extravagant affair to launch a rendezvous in the mountains without an explicit invitation of his presence. Tensions were only heightened when Giuseppe displayed a desire to conquer the slopes of Tahoe. The arrangement of future social outings brought an apprehensive sigh from Bryan still seated next to me on the upper deck. Below us Olive gibbered loudly of how "*we* love skiing," and "Tahoe is *our* favorite place," and so on. For Bryan to be associated with a farce infuriated him. He'd reached a breaking point.

"When we dock I'm going to leave her," he murmured.

"For what?"

There was no reply. Rather, Bryan merely stood up and went inside to where he'd begin packing his things without the surveillance of Olive who remained on the deck, performing her version of the perfect marriage.

The tranquility and anonymity of the sea had staggered Bryan. He'd been placed in a capsule floating through oblivion accompanied by a spectrum of his desires and disgusts, ambitions and ailments, having to choose between the man he was and the man he wanted to be. In many ways he and I were trapped in the same happenstance, attempting to preserve our social standings while trying to forge new experiences we could use as ruminations for our creative endeavors. We were striving to flourish but managing only the basis of survival.

DIATRIBES

It began to rain at noon as the New Florentine penetrated the mass of clouds we'd all been contemplating over. Inside the assemblage was rowdy, as if in defiance of the storm outside or maybe just too inebriated too early in the day.

"The Nobel is the United Nations of literary prizes," I stammered loudly while seating myself at the immense dining room table, a structure that would have sunk many lesser vessels. At the table the group quarreled madly intone, as if in its dying moments, which it was. In a pair of hours we were to dock in San Francisco. The convention of the miserable and bitchy would finally dissolve.

"How lucky we are to be Americans. As if we were Romans during the Roman empire," Ashley professed. Her statement, like mine before it, was mere verbal ejaculation. No one was listening to anyone other than themselves.

"I think next year we'll cruise from Provincetown to Key West," Halston said, fishing for an endorsement. At this moment he was the only person aboard who wanted to repeat such a voyage.

Not until someone, I don't know who, but was a genius for doing so, asked what the role of The Thinker was in the Information Age, we found ourselves timorously buoyed.

"There will always be writers," Giuseppe motioned first. "Who else to tell those who come after us what we had to endure? What we found humorous or distressing."

"But there are ten 24-hour news channels competing to do just that," Katrin jeered. "The written word is dead."

"Television news does not depict humanity, it depicts key events and peculiarities." Bryan continued, "It does not tell the story of those who have no voice."

"Bryan is right." William said, "You can't tell the story of someone's life on television because it is not a captive medium.

People who are watching television are usually doing something else too, like eating dinner or having sex. Maybe both."

"I think what we're all getting at," I said, "is that a writer's influence is becoming increasingly important as the world's media becomes more and more consolidated."

"You've missed it entirely," Olive jived.

"No, I think you have Olive," I shot back. Never was I going to back down from such a manipulative and insubordinate being.

"Your argument is baseless," she lamented. "Writers don't matter anymore! *You* don't matter anymore."

"I don't matter now anymore than I ever did. But if you'd listen I could explain," I said.

"Explain away!" she finally allowed.

"We keep comparing our work to that of other artists. Of all the art forms that can be reproduced on a mass scale, ours is the most potent. Whereas films are visions of many, many people, such as the screenwriter, the producer, director, studio, financiers… the producer's wife, the director's kid… and so on. The same thing goes with musical artists today where you have giant teams of producers creating the illusion of a musical brilliance and style. But literature - *good* literature - is the one medium where a single voice can stand in equivalence with these other mediums."

"What about painting?" Giuseppe queried.

"Talk about a dead art form!" Katrin burst.

"I resent that," Giuseppe replied, his strongest and most visible confrontation with anyone on the boat yet. "Paintings are interpreted. Novels are digested."

"Isn't this the same conversation we had when we left Seattle?" Ashley noted.

"Cyclicality!" Katrin rooted.

"We write history but do not determine it," Halston grasped. "We are the means of conveyance but not the conveyance!"

"But what is a writer's *worth* today?" Tom asked.

"Depends on who they are," Olive shallowly decided.

"I think what he means to ask is," I said, "whether or not a writer's contribution to society is on par with say, someone working in a factory?"

This is when William Zofield piped in with his own diatribe. "In no other industry does someone working on their craft see such a long period of delayed gratification between conceptualization and fruition. Many of us write for years before we see a check, read a review or are given an opinion from a reader. And of course, there are those who never experience such things because their ideas are too large to grasp in just one lifetime. They write their entire lives, composing manuscript after manuscript, and out of laziness or disinterest, never get published. Their works lie unknown, possibly forever, in a realm of vast anonymity. Their voices muted forever."

"I completely agree," Tom endorsed. "I've always thought that some of the greatest novels ever written were likely never published because their authors were writers, not salesmen."

"The purpose of writing is neither fame nor notoriety," Olive sneered. Paradoxically, she had a supple allocation of both of these benefits. It was the same kind of insipid comment rich people often used to illustrate the unimportance of wealth.

Never one to stand in pure concurrence with a crowd, and especially her father, Katrin argued, "It is true many writer's write for fame and notoriety, but their sincere purpose is to communicate. If no one is reading what you've written you're communicating with no one but yourself. And that's just merely therapy."

"If we're trying to determine what the public, as in the masses, consider the value of a writer to be," I said, "one must take in to account the variable of a person's value of new ideas and intellectual concepts."

"Exactly!" William proclaimed. "Commoners and we literati have two very different appreciations for the idea. Most people would consider a story as something you buy, not something you create."

"And many people believe," Tom alleged, "that reading stories is a waste of time. Most people in this country do not read on a regular basis. Books and the people who read them are looked down on in many circles as something only those attempting to assert their elitism use."

"You're drunk!" Olive blasted, she herself queasier and more intoxicated than anyone else. "Everybody reads! Don't make it sound like everyone is stupid and only the decidedly academic have the intellect to pick up a book. It's so... last century... no, it's so Victorian."

"Everybody reads?" Tom fired back. "Gossip websites and popular scandal magazines do not count as reading, Olive."

"It's not as if your books are entirely literary Tom! That last one of yours, what was it? Fifty-thousand words? Not exactly Moby Dick. Hell, it wasn't even the abridged version of Dick."

"It's not the size of the novel that matters," I mediated, "but the ideas expressed within it that are of greatest importance."

"Why do I get the overwhelming sense this isn't the first time you've defended the size of your novels," Olive cackled. Some of the others laughed meekly along with her. I wasn't sure if they were laughing at her gag or the ass she was making of herself.

Giuseppe, the only one who was not drinking and did not appear to be amused by the sizzling backbiting, brought the group's deliberation back in to session with the question: "Could it be estimated that many of the world's readers are disgusted with literature because it is so often used for agenda pushing or propagandizing."

"That's an incredibly important question," William snapped.

"I read the question in a *People* magazine article last night. I'm not sure what it means."

"Well," William sighed as he stood up, "I'm off to go kill myself." This meant he was going to his bedroom to take one of his naps. For the duration of the pleasure cruise William had napped on average twice a day, always post-breakfast and post-lunch. With the absence of Zofield came a familiar silence. Without the presence of the one mind that could either validate or quell the egos and ideas of us writers, no one seemed to care to share their grandiose concepts. Topics of converse reverted to the weather and, ugh, sports. The silence became nearly unbearable when Tom asked if anyone had heard who was winning the American League playoffs.

"Where are you headed after San Francisco?" I asked Halston while the others were on the topic of self-publishing and the inability to make money off the effort.

"We," he said, referring to himself and Giuseppe, "are off to Europe. We're going to sail down the Baja, zip through the canal and mosey on over to the Mediterranean to spend a couple nights along the Cote d'Azur. After that, who knows!"

When Halston said this I could see discomfort in Giuseppe's face. It was a look of doubt, of reluctance and pity. I knew then what Halston did not. Giuseppe was going to leave him when we reached San Francisco. Earlier that morning I'd seen the young man discreetly packing a suitcase in his bedroom, the one he kept separate from his rich lover. The event, at the time, had not shocked me as everyone was packing things. But in my brief observation noticed Giuseppe was packing things one would take if he were not to return to the ship, like pictures, candles and towels. Everything he owned fit in to one standard suitcase weighing surely no more than forty pounds. He was a true 21st-Century nomad and I envied him.

A PASSING

With fanfare, the New Florentine's captain announced we were a mere hour from entering San Francisco Bay. This broadcast roused me from a gentle slumber. In tidying my suite, not wanting to leave one trace of ingratitude behind, I'd fallen asleep on top of the bed I'd just spent ten painstaking minutes making. In waking I found I already had my shoes on and my hand outstretched to one of the suitcases next to the bed. I was unquestionably prepared to return home, though I was at the time fooling around with the idea of checking in to the Fairmont for a day or two with the intention of rediscovering San Francisco. For all the times I'd visited the city I always suspected I was missing something. San Francisco was a city of many layers and I'd only seen the surface.

I went to the hallway and approached the staircase leading up to the foredeck when I heard the voice of Katrin coming from William's suite. Unable to make out her full sentences, I could tell from her tone she was ridiculing her father unless the phrases "foolish bastard" and "jealous fucker" were terms of endearment she used for him. I tapped on the door and went in.

"Marc!" Katrin said with a glowering sniffle. She was surprised to see me. I was stunned to find her wiping away a stream of tears while hovering over William, still napping.

"Are you alright?" I asked. Upon my approach of her she stood up and gestured for me not to come any closer.

"I'm fine. I should have seen this coming. I should have known."

I presumed she was upset to be leaving the New Florentine. I didn't care for the drama, but some people, like Katrin, thrived on such interactions. Conflict galvanized their convictions and fueled their ambition.

"He's such a selfish, selfish prick," she cried again.

"Why, what happened? What did he say?" I asked. I'd never known her to use such slander toward her father, no matter how much adolescent respite she still had for him.

"He killed himself," she sobbed and then sat back down next to William's body, grasping her face of tears in her hands. I then noticed several empty bottles of prescription pain killers and anti-depressants next to the bed, alongside a nearly full glass of water. A crumpled piece of paper lay on the floor. Her mourning was for a departure of a different sort.

I picked the crumpled letter up off the floor, flattened it and read the suicidal manifesto. In it William described how proud he was of his daughter and what an inspiration she was. He also remarked how much she was like her mother in all her nuances and that every moment he spent with was like spending time with his deceased wife reincarnate. He described the pain he felt for not publishing a work in three decades and how useless and annoyed he was living in the shadow of the recently deceased William Zolinsky, an English playwright he was often confused with in the press and in person. They even bore not just similar names but a physical resemblance of tall, stocky and balding. The last line of the note read: "in time you will find my magnum opus." I took this to mean that people would find his work, some of it tragically out of print, to increase in importance upon his death.

"Did you read this?" I asked Katrin as softly as I could.

"I don't have to," she roared.

"It says he loves you very much."

"I know he does," she solemnly acknowledged. I then witnessed a transformation in Katrin. Her sadness evaporated within the second when she came to realize her life was now alleviated by the burden her father had always been to her. At once she became upbeat, pensive, alert, and controlling. She'd been planning the eventual death of her father for some time, as every child should do just as one plans one's own retirement.

"I'll fly directly to London when we get to shore. His house will take some time to get in order, but it will sell fast."

"You waste no time," I blurted.

"I've wasted too much already. He was dead to me a long time ago. Now we can both move on."

"You sound so cold," I replied, to which she sighed tumultuously.

"You don't understand me," she hissed. "And you certainly didn't know my father. He was a cruel man. Selfish, disillusioned, broken… just like so many men are today."

I didn't say anything in return. I just watched Katrin as she worked, collecting her dead father's clothes from the closet and shoving them in to one of the large trunks he'd brought with him.

"See how selfish he is!" she erupted. "He could have at least packed his shit up before leaving us. But no! I have to do it. Just like I always do. Thanks *dad*."

It did not occur to her there were staff on the ship willing, capable, and intended to perform such tasks. To Katrin this sloppiness was just another example of William's obtuse senility.

"Well at least he remembered this," Katrin winced as she unfolded a set of papers taped to William's dresser next to his wallet and spare change.

"What's that?" I asked. She said it was his last will and testament. In it William requested he be cremated immediately without autopsy and his ashes scatted about the grounds of the Palace of Fine Arts in none other than San Francisco.

"His death was opportunistic," I said.

"Yes," Katrin agreed. Brazenly sardonic, she added, "I'm sure he said 'Since I'm going to San Francisco I might as well kill myself!'"

"Why the Palace?" I asked. "You'd think he'd want to be scattered someplace in London."

"Or even Brussels… he loves Brussels," Katrin pondered until she realized the significance of the museum. "He met my mother at the Palace of Fine Arts. They were both tourists who kept bumping in to each other all over the city one weekend. It was at the Palace she asked him out on a date."

"She asked him?" I raised.

"Yes. It was during the peak of the sexual revolution, or so the story goes."

"What better way to return to the sight of where you met your one true love?"

"Yes, as a burnt up corpse!"

Katrin was humbled by her father's last wish. It was something she did not expect from him as she questioned many times over since the death of her mother if William had ever really loved her. Everyone knew, because he was famous for it, that William had mistresses. According to the most abhorrent biographers these lovers were often of both sexes, a fact William never bothered to contest.

"Are you going to be alright?" I asked Katrin, preparing to leave her with William and his things.

"I'm fine," she said convincingly assured. "Just help me move his shit out in the hallway. I don't want the staff to be subjected to this scene."

"I'm sure they've seen worse," I said, poking fun at Halston's reputation. This allowed Katrin to have an easing, if not brief and incongruous chuckle.

Next to the armoire was William's largest case, one I was sure Katrin would find immovable.

"Christ this is heavy!" I exclaimed, attempting to lift the giant thing.

"It's probably the case of tequila he bought at the duty free."

"No," I replied, "he already drank that one."

"You don't think he stole anything do you?" she asked.

"Why would he?"

"He's a kleptomaniac!"

Immediately she unlocked the case, disturbed knowing her father, even in his final days, maintained a proclivity for thievery. However, it was not bone china, paintings, or silverware that fell out of the case, but reams worth of paper. There were thousands of pages, many of them wrinkled and dog eared, all of them unpublished Zofield work. It was work no one who knew him could have known existed. Those closest to William Zofield believed him to be retired from writing. Nowhere in his home was their proof of such an act as writing; he owned neither a typewriter nor a computer. What made this discovery all the more astonishing was Zofield had written, by hand, each of the words on each of the thousands of pages. It was stealthy and ingenious for him to resort to such primitive means of composition. Had he maintained a writer's domain of desk, chair, paper, computer, printer, et al, surely one of his acquaintances would have expected something to materialize from the environment in which he inhabited. But because he'd composed his prose in secret without the eager eyes of bystanders, a hampering bi-product so many prized writers find to be the most intimidating aspect of penning sequential works, William had found freedom in the arena in which he labored. He was without an audience, agent, or editor. No one questioned "how's the novel coming?" because no one knew of a novel to be in the making.

"These can't be worth anything," Katrin asserted as she opened the first manuscript. She then read the first page of the book she ridiculed and continued on to the next, fully rapt. Eventually she took a seat on the bed next to her dead father, reading his final passages of a fictional nature, captivated as anyone who might ever have read a book.

DINOSAURS

Verdi's *Ell Mi Fu Rapita* resounded madly from a symphonic array of tiny speakers within the New Florentine's library as I entered it searching for Halston. At his desk in front of his computer I found him deeply engrossed, working on his newest novel of drivel, tentatively titled *Gentlemen Prefer Boys*.

"Marc!" he shouted over the opera, "I'm so happy you're here. You're a walking thesaurus. What's a fanciful term for anus?"

I thought for a moment and said, "Firmly puckered gloriousness."

"Perfect," he said and continued writing. "Makes it sound delicious."

"Halston," I interrupted him, "I have to tell you something."

"I already know Marc. I don't need any observations from you. Observations are really just judgments disguised as assistance, but they are what they are," he rambled. I hadn't a clue what he was talking about.

"Zofield has killed himself," I blunted.

Halston gasped and rubbed his throat as if it had clenched itself shut and he couldn't breathe. But then he said, "Really? On my ship! Here, right now!" All of this uttered in a morbid delight, as if he was proud to have been in some way associated with such a momentous event. After all, it's not every day England's... no, *Europe's* most notorious novelist does himself in.

"It wasn't with a gun was it?" Halston queried, worrying foremost for his upholstery and linens.

"No. Pills," I replied.

Halston exhaled with relief. "Where's the body?"

"In his room, in his bed. He looks like he's sleeping."

"I'll have the captain call the shore," Halston said excitedly as though anticipating a fiendish event, which he was. Halston could not have asked for a more prestigious happening to take place on this late summer outing. The death of a renowned writer via something as quixotic as suicide could only add to the lustrous shine of the literary echelon of which he wished to form. Surely Halston considered the death of the Great Zofield to be in every newspaper in every country which published his work, along with the obligatory biography of life and work, as well as the telling of where and how the writer died. Halston could read the news print in his mind:

Famed English writer and social commentator William Zofield died aboard Halston Levy's New Florentine yacht today while attending a summit of the world's greatest writers. Zofield is the author of over 30 novels, including Rapture, The Countess of California, *and* Mahogany. *The cause of death, still to be determined by officials in San Francisco, is said to be the result of an intentional ingestion of a large dose of various prescription medications. William Zofield's daughter Katrin, author of the post-feminist classic* Womanhattan, *who was among the passengers, said of her father in an interview immediately after leaving the luxury vessel, "Dad was a noble, brilliant, fragile man who couldn't tolerate the cruelty in which he found the world. He will be missed."*

"Where are the others?" I asked Halston as he stared in to nothingness, contemplating this turn of events.

"They're out front. We're approaching the bridge."

The premature autumn had immersed San Francisco with a foggy chill. Despite the weather, it was unable to deter some from anticipating the view of the Golden Gate. On the ship's deck Tom and Ashley stood clustered together sharing an ice cream cone. Giuseppe and Bryan joked about how the ship could crash in to Alcatraz because of the thick fog. Olive, alone at the railing, peered down at the water gliding along the hull.

"Everyone, please come inside," Halston beckoned.

"We'll miss the bridge!" Ashley protested. Her retort and the reception of the other callous faces prompted me to blurt out the news.

"William Zofield has killed himself," I said.

"How sensational!" Ashley jeered. Some people handle death strangely.

"That's horrible to say," Olive flamed. "How's Katrin?"

Olive didn't wait for my reply before leaving the deck to go find Katrin and console her. The others were stunned but the shock dissipated quickly when the death was realized to be the perfect end to both a stagnate career and rapidly deteriorating life.

"Where's the body?" Tom asked after huddling next to me.

"In his room. Katrin is packing his things."

"Was she crying?"

"Yes. Briefly," I replied, "but I think she is happy for him in a way. The suffering has come to an end."

"Suffering?" Ashley quizzed, joining our cluster. "The man seemed rather jolly to me."

"He had many demons. It's no wonder he killed himself," I said.

"Or she killed him," Tom added. I laughed at his proposal until I recognized he was being entirely frank. "That can't be it!" Tom bellowed as the underbelly of the bridge, discolored by pollution and corrosion, pierced through the sea's dismal miasma.

"It's so small," Tom sniffed.

"Isn't everything man creates a disappointment?" Ashley replied.

No one responded to her. Humor, especially the black humor in which she discharged, did not fit the moment. Instead we all glared at the aloft bridge, watching as it glided over us and sank in to the same mist it emerged from. To some it was glorious, to others the weather had unjustly skewed and defaced its grandeur. To me, it was just a goddamn bridge.

After passing the Golden Gate everyone immediately went inside to collect their luggage and gifts and to say farewell. In the ship's main lounge everyone but Katrin and Olive hugged and laughed at the abrupt discomfort of knowing there was a corpse onboard. Then the topic turned to speculation as to whether or not the San Francisco police would be performing an investigation.

"Do you think we'll be detained?" Giuseppe asked, already in search of his visa.

"Who knows? They have no reason to believe it wasn't suicide," Ashley gulped.

"Halston, did you alert the press?" I asked.

"No. I called the county sheriff to tell them what happened. They said they would send someone to the pier to meet us. But you know how the cops are these days! They're in it with the tabloids."

Everyone began talking at once of how they'd react to a swarm of media if such a thing should be present at the pier when we docked. Olive and Katrin entered the room shortly thereafter and at once wanted to know what the commotion was about.

"The newspapers and televisions cameras might be at the dock," Tom announced favorably. Of all the minor celebrities aboard he was the only one with extensive time spent in front of television cameras. It was customary for Tom Reynolds to appear on *The Today Show* and countless other morning gigs every time he published a new book.

With only a few moments before they were to be cast in to what they considered to be the glaring spotlight of notoriety, each member of the group rethought what it was they wore and how they'd done their hair. Most everyone would try to covertly examine themselves in a mirror, as nonchalantly as possible, not wanting the others to witness their narcissism or assume any sort anticipation for recognition. Katrin would reapply her flawless makeup and Halston would add a handsome jacket to his attire. I'll admit I examined my own reflection in the vase on the table next to where I sat, eagerly anticipating our docking.

"I've arranged for some cars to take us to the Fairmont," Halston announced. "Everyone has a suite there waiting for them. I thought we could, if at all possible, have one last dinner together before we all go our separate ways." Everyone welcomed the idea, including myself. The atmosphere on the New Florentine had become so overcast and toxic I thought it gallant of Mr. Levy to arrange a restorative collaboration in some place as sovereign as a hotel.

A moment later we trampled along the historic pier, lined with antiquated ships such as the Eureka ferry and the well-kept Scottish Balchlutha, each of them now serving as museums to seafaring days gone by. Other than a sprinkling of wandering tourists and a single white cargo van parked on the street, the side of it marked San Francisco County Coroner in small black letters across the back, the pier was desolate. No photographers. Not a single scribe from one of the city's many newspapers or literary journals made an appearance. The regular flow of tourists who usually dotted the pier weren't anywhere to be found. Even they found us and our dead colleague to be of little concern.

"There's a writer's worth for you!" I heard Giuseppe cackle as he walked behind me. He and I could both sense the resonant disappoint the other writers were undergoing. For no member of the press to appear at the scene of death of a once great writer was preposterous. Certainly, had the corpse in the New Florentine been that of a professional athlete or minor television personality, we'd have been inundated with photographers and pleading media representatives. But because William Zofield was a writer, a person society viewed as obsolete, as it did the boats which lined the Hyde Street pier, which were maintained in order to function but cruelly never put to work, the wholesalers of news and entertainment looked for other trashy bits of gossip and misfortune to exploit. On this day the national papers and television news channels publicized the trial of a man accused of killing his pregnant wife and dumping her in the same bay we'd just floated in on.

Waiting for us at the pier's gates were a league of black limousines. Halston didn't even skimp on the ground transportation. The ship's crew quickly loaded everyone's things in to their corresponding car. Words of thanks and gratitude were now postponed for the after-cruise reception to be held at the hotel later in the evening.

"Where are the police?" Halston asked one of the men sitting in the coroner's van.

"Did you call them?" the man replied.

"I called the sheriff, told them a man killed himself on my boat."

"So what do you need the police for?" one of the men replied dully.

"Aren't they involved in these sorts of things?"

"The police don't care if some old dude ODs out in the ocean," the same man retorted dryly. "This is San Francisco… The police have real problems to worry about, like crime."

As the others briskly loaded in to their limos and readied themselves for departure, Katrin and I stayed and watched the men unload a gurney from the back of the van and wheel it down the pier toward the yacht where the captain of the ship, a man who'd remained entirely unseen by us the entire length of the cruise, suddenly emerged to take care of the dirty business.

"Can you believe that?" I asked Katrin. "They don't investigate these things anymore."

"If I knew that I would have killed him myself a long time ago," she said. It was not out of cruelty she said this. For if I were to rephrase her statement to its most punctual form I'd have it include something about William being a miserable creature who was only doing the right thing in ending his life. Certainly few would agree that suicide is ever the correct path to take one's life down, but in William's case I believe it will enhance the tragedy of his work historically by putting an explanation point at the end of his biography. He was a man who festered in self-loathing and despair. Those kinds of writers tend to live forever in legend. This event would finally give him and his impressive body of work the emphasis and attention it always deserved but never truly received outside of literary circles.

In an eerily synchronized procession, each of the dark sedans pulled away from the marina leaving me there with Katrin. Being alone with her for the first time off the yacht prompted a sensation of regeneration. We could start over now, away from our associates and friends, to do what we wished and be as we pleased. It was in moments like this where the realization that one appreciates being an artist - a person who does not inhabit an office, punch a time clock, nor report to a superior – that the feeling of true freedom is of its greatest magnitude.

"What do we do now?" Katrin asked me.

"I can't think of anything," I replied listlessly, having failed to contemplate what I'd do when we arrived in San Francisco.

"I don't know what to do about that," she said, pointing to the suitcase containing William's manuscripts.

"I'd be very careful. In the wrong hands they could seriously taint your father's legacy."

"Are you staying in San Francisco very long? I could use your help. I can't go back to New York now. Not with what has happened." Her plea was timid and desperate.

"What can I do?" I asked. As awkward and sudden as the moment was, I didn't want Katrin to feel like I, a man who'd shared certain intimacies with her, maybe as a means of furthering my writing, was going to abandon her the moment things turned grim or uncomfortable.

"Make sure I'm not a fool. Make sure I don't sell these things to the highest bidder."

We walked to the car and I put my arm around her. "I'm sorry, but the grapes are waiting," I said, intending this to be our last words but she grasped my hand, preventing me from getting in the car. She began apologizing.

"I'm sorry Marc. I know I shut you out, but you don't understand me. I can't take care of people. It's just not me! It's why I've never had kids. It's why I've never had a husband. You men all just want mothers and I can't be a mother. I wasn't made like that. I don't have that gene."

"Nobody does," I replied, "caring for others is something you learn."

"Marc," she scowled, "you really don't understand women."

"I know," I countered, "if I did my life would be a lot simpler than it is."

Her silence made me believe she found this statement amusing.

"Will I see you at the hotel?" I asked.

"No. I've got to get dad cremated and find the Palace of Fine Arts," she said. I kissed her on the cheek, said goodbye, and I got in the car. As my sedan drove away I could see Katrin standing alone on the dock watching as the two men wheeled her father's loosely draped body up the pier and loaded him to their waiting van. I did not feel sorry for her as much as I pitied her. She was the only person in the world who would never be able to tally the worth of her father. Few children grow up with the privilege of having such an accomplished intellectual in the family whose name is able to grant admission to any college, or whose money could have prevented her from ever having to maintain a living. She was born without obligation. It was she who'd created the wealth of her problems, not her father. To leave Katrin there, alone, with the grief she'd created was a fortune to cherish. We'd shared each other physically but not in any other way. We couldn't ever build on it as what it was based on, loneliness, was as brittle a foundation as lust.

SPECIAL RELATIONSHIP

The Fairmont is San Francisco's grande dame of temporary residence rightly perched atop Nob Hill. So regal, the place could easily double as the consulate of a major nation or ritzy department store. I love staying in places like these. They make me feel so important. Well, more important than I already consider myself.

Of course I was the last to arrive but nonetheless was joined in the lobby by the other stragglers, Bryan Madden, Halston Levy, Giuseppe Tavolo, and Olive Snow. Tom Reynolds and Ashley Mulberry were also present, though they were still checking in, trading their two separate rooms for a single bay view suite.

Given the jolly mood everyone was in I figured they'd forgotten about the self-inflicted demise of their fellow traveler.

"Good evening Mulberry," Olive jested.

"Hello. What are the plans?"

"You're in room 401," Halston said, handing me the key to the room. "Dinner is at seven. We're eating here at the hotel. They just hired the most wonderful chef from Tokyo."

"Can't wait," I replied.

Tom and Ashley, sickeningly entwined in each other's arms like the salatious lovers they aspired to be, came over to join the rest of us.

"How's Katrin?" Ashley asked me.

"She seems fine," I said. This was followed by a gangly silence, so I added, "She's handling it well."

As the seven of us began determining just what our plans for the rest of the evening would be, a world-famous male movie star stormed raucously in to the hotel with entourage and paparazzi hauled behind him. Ordinary people, who you'd never expect of going star bonkers, like businessmen, ladies who lunch and hotel employees, did just that. They clamored for an autograph and a picture with the massive, brilliant star. One lady of an elderly disposition fainted and fell in to a potted plant when she realized who the celebrity was. Luckily the concierge was nearby to revive her. When she repeated her fainting spell, this time more flagrantly and in closer proximity to the celebrity, I assumed she was doing it to catch his sympathy, and an autograph.

The movie star noticed Bryan Madden immediately. Bryan was unaware of the commotion the celebrity had summoned as he was involved in an argument with his wife over whether or not to hit the town after dinner.

"Madden!" the movie star hailed. Bryan turned to witness the film star's entourage shooing away fans and gawkers in order for him to have a private conversation, but it was no good. Even as Bryan introduced his wife to the man people continued to take their picture with him and he would, without acknowledging them, continue to sign autographs on whatever they held up for him. One woman even proposed he sign her infant baby but someone from the hotel staff escorted her to the exit.

"Everyone, this is…" Bryan introduced us to the star, needlessly. "These are my friends," he then introduced each of us. The celebrity, a dimwit, knew none of our names, not even mine, which I deemed ironic considering he'd played a starring role in the film adaptation of my first novel.

"It's very nice to meet all of you," the actor gushed falsely, proving he was not worthy of the Academy Award he'd won for his portrayal of a philandering Spanish painter. "I'm so intimidated…" he added falsely, "you're all so accomplished."

The star took Bryan aside and began to speak to him as though they were two boys on the same football team. From examining them I knew there was more than a simple acquaintanceship between them. The star was genuinely captivated by Bryan. If he'd been acting I'm sure he would have come off as simply mocking captivation because the actor was nowhere near subtle in his technique – after all, this was a man known for fiery onscreen raging tantrums, not restrained nuances. Bryan's reaction to this attention was nothing less than that of gushy, warm delight.

"They must be good friends," I said to Olive.

"Old friends," she said, then restated, "inseparable *old* friends."

Ashley, born with the same intuition I was graciously blessed, arrived at the same assumption I had seeing the two men talk with each other. "Looks like a lovers spat," she said, now referencing the movie star with his hand on his hip while Bryan tried to explain the presence of his wife and his obligation to spend time exclusively with her. Not to be kept waiting, the star, after huffing and using a very animated finger to illustrate his disappointment with Bryan, pivoted and exited the hotel, paparazzi outside snapping his every haughty gesture.

"These damn drama queens," Bryan cursed as he returned to our circle. "They want everything."

"Are you two working on something together?" Tom asked, his question loaded with delicious insinuation.

"No. Not yet. He wants thirty-million for my next project, the one that's supposed to be a return to gritty, bare-bones filmmaking."

"Sounds hot," Ashley bantered.

"Why not give it to him?" Halston asked. "He fills theaters. That last one of his made a billion dollars!"

"Yeah, but he's a pain to work with. Excuse me, pain to work *for*. As many demands as he makes you'd think the producers were paid by him. Anyway, everyone in the business says he's past his prime and I'm starting to believe them."

"Isn't that the same thing they say about you dear?" Olive unexpectedly seared him.

"Honey!" Bryan cried.

"I'm just saying don't discount someone's talent because of what others say about them."

"I'd like to know who it is that says I'm past my prime!" The two queer married liars continued their spat as a team of bellhops caravanned the posse's luggage toward the elevator.

"Marc!" I heard bawled across the echoing marble lobby – to which several other men, presumably sharing a name, turned their heads to look. The shriek came from someone I hadn't spoken to in months but couldn't have been more delighted to see: the former Mrs. Mulberry, Amelia Haughton.

"She's a day early," Ashley said with blight as Amelia approached our group. She carried a small tote and dressed in whatever was the hottest thing in New York. Skin being out at the moment, she was draped in about a mile of flowing Italian floral silk, sunglasses, and her hair up as high as it could be wrapped and stuffed in a clouche.

"I thought it'd be a clever little arrangement. But I see now it was foolish," Ashley scolded herself.

"What are you talking about? This is great," I replied.

Amelia hugged me like French snobs do, with her folded arms reaching around me no further than the top of my shoulders.

"I can't believe you're here! What are you doing here?" she was flabbergasted. It felt decadent to enchant someone so fully.

"It's the end of Halston's yearly cruise," I said. She then glimpsed over at Halston and shrieked upon seeing him.

"Oh my lord Hal, you're a gorgeous hunk!" she exclaimed, hugging him much more vigorously than she did me. "You've lost so much weight," she added in a whisper, then teased him by poking his abdomen and declaring "good god! You have abs! Where did you buy them?"

In the elevator I introduced everyone who didn't already know Amelia, which turned out to be only Giuseppe and Bryan. By no coincidence Amelia's suite was next door to mine and before I could invite her to have a pre-cocktail hour drink in my room I found myself in hers, reminiscing about the "marriage that got away," as she referred to it.

"I feel so selfish Marc!" she proclaimed while digging through the ice bucket trying to find the perfect cubes for our gin and tonics.

"Selfish?" I laughed, "I was the one who wouldn't leave my house to visit you. It was I who demanded privacy from eight AM to noon. I pushed you away. It's obvious to me now."

"No! I knew going in to it you were a hermit. I'd read all the articles about you and your method of complete isolationism.

That's what attracted me to you. As if you were a rare treasure to be hunted and then cherished when found."

"It must have been strange going back."

"Back to what?"

"To New York. I remember for a while you seemed happy in the country. At one with it. Like you'd found yourself."

Amelia handed me my cocktail and we sat in front of the window, both of us absorbing the late day's sunset and the inescapable aura of San Francisco and its glistening bay. On such beautiful evenings I'm not sure there is a more picturesque location on Earth.

"Yes, I admit I learned something out there on that island of yours. But how many times does a person need to find themselves?"

"I suppose, every time they lose themselves," I said. "You don't miss it?"

"Sometimes. Like when I'm sitting in a cab on Park Avenue and there are cars and people everywhere yet nobody is moving and I'm running late and I have to be somewhere or I'll die, only whatever it is I'm going to doesn't matter and I just want to escape."

"So escape," glancing at her. "I'd love to have you by the house sometime." Her eyes met mine for a moment. Her instinct was to pull her eyes away from mine and the moment she did she recanted and brought them back to me.

"I couldn't do that," she flushed, looking away again.

"Why not? Those douglas fir trees you planted are behemouths. Skyscrapers even," I tried to lure her. I believed she dreamt of such a retreat, if only for old time's sake.

"Although, the girls in the office were quite fascinated when I mentioned life on the vineyard."

"Girls? I thought you said *Vanity Fair* was overwhelmingly male?"

"I left *VF* for *W* about nine months ago. You'd know that if we ever kept in touch." I instantly assumed she knew Katrin Zofield.

"It's a two-way street babe."

"I'm not blaming you. I'm just saying if we ever talked we'd know more about each other. Like, how's this year's vintage?" She asked this with absolute sincerity. The winemaking function of my estate was one of only two things she ever took any interest in. Her other interest, me, was one she'd grown tired of not long after we were married and my persnickety nature became known to her.

"The best yet," I said. "It's humongous. You wouldn't believe how many grapes we get now. The vines have matured robustly. You should see the cellars. The barrels are stacked five high and go back fourteen rows."

"What about your books?" she delicately raised. "I read the last one of yours. I'd say it was a commendable redemption for that piece of trash *Pike Street*, but what's next?"

"I'm blocked right now."

"You poor thing. Have you gone back to Italy?" It was not unlike Amelia to be so consoling. I missed that the most about her.

"I'm thinking about it." This was an understatement. The truth was I thought about it every day, regretting I hadn't already been there and back a hundred times. For whatever reason, I put Italy off just like I did my writing. They were both things I wanted to do and knew I should, but I just didn't. For some inexplicable reason I was unable to do what I knew was right.

"You should go," Amelia purred. "It stirs something in you."

"I know. You're absolutely right. It's strange to meet someone who knows so much about me. You haven't forgotten a thing, have you?"

"No I haven't. But you know..." she paused, cackling with humility, "I admit it! I sometimes still refer to you as my husband! I'm so ridiculous like that. As if you were my husband in storage... or in waiting."

"It's been four years," I said. We both laughed awkwardly. We had both failed to move on with our lives. And now we were bonding because of that.

"I know, I'm crazy. But I think it's because we shared something many husbands and wives don't. And honestly, there aren't very many people in this world who really know you Marc. And sometimes I feel I don't even know you that well, you have so many layers it's hard to grasp who you really are. You perplex me still."

"You and me both. I haven't a clue where I'm headed right now. The passion to write has been gone for so long."

"Don't worry about it. When you put expectations and deadlines on things it only makes it more of a chore than a pleasure. And if all else fails, retire! You've certainly made a large enough name for yourself to do that with some grace."

"Not a bad idea."

"If you were to retire I'd think you'd find the passion to write again. Wouldn't you agree that writing seems to just pour out more freely when it's random and unexpected. Like sex."

"It's absolutely like sex," I affirmed.

"That reminds me, I should tell you how good you look. I'd say well-rested, but I know that face."

"What face?"

"You've been getting laid. Or you've had plastic surgery."

"I haven't had any plastic surgery," I replied, then snickered with selfish glee.

"With who has it been with? It wasn't Halston was it?" she ribbed back.

"No. It was with…" I hesitated in order to garner my discretion, "Katrin Zofield."

"Oh!" Amelia exclaimed in disbelief. "She asked me about you before she left last week. Told me she was going to have sex with you. I told her you weren't her type. But I guess types change." She held up her cocktail as if to cheer me, and swallowed what remained.

"She said that? Women tell each other things like that?" As far as I knew it was unlike Amelia to discuss sex openly with others. She was one of the most modest of modern women I knew. Like tastes, people's discretion appeared to change with time too.

"Yes. We have our conquests just as you men do."

"And you tell each other of them?"

"Certainly. It's not much of a triumph if one cannot gloat in the revelry of other's jealousy."

"I suppose if you're in to that." A creeping sense of disgust came over me knowing that two women had planned and plotted bedding me. I considered what they must have said about me. Did they deem me such an easy lay that they could predict I would bed any woman who dropped her panties in my presence?

"Speaking of what people are in to, Ashley told me you had some sort of curious rendezvous with Bryan Madden. That man is a homosexual. Everyone sees it except his wife."

"Are you sure she doesn't?"

"Who knows! Let's stop talking about other people."

"Why? Because it's so much more fascinating when we talk solely about ourselves?"

"What time is it?"

"Twenty minutes until dinner," I replied.

Trying to keep up with Amelia, I finished my drink. She dashed back to her hotel room to get dressed. Moments later Amelia and I reunited in the hotel's restaurant lobby where we were told by the hostess that dinner had been cancelled. Apparently Halston was ill and could not attend. However, the absence of the man who'd been masterminding every meal and ceremony I'd been a part of for the last four days only encouraged me to have dinner, especially now since the woman I started to feel something for once more was suddenly by my side.

"You have to tell me all about the cruise. Was it absolute debauchery?" Amelia asked, unenthused but interested just in case there was a scandal brewing.

"Yes. There was booze, whores and donuts everywhere. Everything one needs to be a debaucher nowadays."

The hostess sat us in a candlelit booth big enough for six people, which in some strange way was able to make the seating arrangement feel all the more intimate.

"Wish I could have attended," she said jokingly.

"That's unheard of. He doesn't invite those who are not vain, self-important egoists."

"No. But ex-wives of vain, self-important egoists are allowed as stowaways, aren't they?"

"They are, yes. But you would have hated it. I hated it. So boring. So nauseating."

"I would have assumed you'd enjoy the solace of the sea."

"*Solace of the sea*," I repeated in examination. I then recalled where I'd heard the phrase before. "You stole that from Halston. That's how he described his fascination with boating in his memoir, *HL*. He wrote an entire 88-page chapter about the blossoming literary scene in Seattle he left so he could navigate desolate, endless oceans.

"I'm a lifter. I take things. Authors should be flattered when people do that."

"Shut it you plagiarist slut," I jabbered, feeling the full wrath of my cocktail.

"What are you doing reading Halston Levy? You always dismissed his work as gay Harlequin."

"I did a piece on the emerging influence of gay writers in popular literature. Gay Harlequin is the new female porn. Something about it makes lonely 40-something-year-old women moist. And it beats watching QVC alone all night."

"How fascinating," I replied dryly.

"What? You read it and you're pissed he didn't give you a mention?"

"That's enough. I'm already in the midst of a sexual identity crisis." The moment I admitted a weakness or doubt Amelia would swoop in to defend and undo any harm she caused, as she did this same evening.

"Oh my! Baby, what's the matter?" she soothed.

"It's nothing. But, as you insinuated, I did have a questionable encounter with Bryan Madden."

"Enough!" she intervened. "I don't want to hear about it. No matter how lurid it was, it doesn't matter. I just can't imagine you humping another man. When it comes to sex you're..." she searched for the precise word, "delicate."

"Jesus Christ Amelia!" I exploded.

"I hate it when you use that expression. You don't even believe in Jesus."

"Ok, but there was no humping. And what do you mean by *delicate?*" I demanded clarification, assuming she was calling me a pansy in bed.

"Gentle. That's what I meant," she retracted. "Every woman's dream."

"Speaking of gentle," I said, "Bryan Madden knew what he was doing. He could teach a fellatio class."

"Stop! I don't want to hear about it," she screeched, but then retreated "...really?"

"Yes, he was an expert. Katrin could have learned a few things from him."

"All I'll say is that it's not like perfectly straight people don't veer to the other side of the road every now and then. For instance, back at Wellesley I let one of the girls in my economics class tongue me in the back of a pickup truck when I was drunk."

"I know, you've told me that story a hundred-thousand times. As though you're proud of it."

The waiter came by and asked us if we were ready to order. We'd been so preoccupied by topics of nastiness we'd forgotten our purpose in the restaurant. Amelia shooed the waiter away explaining she still had no idea what she wanted.

"Nothing sounds good," Amelia pouted as she flipped through her menu.

"I'm not even hungry," I said.

"Me neither. Let's ditch this place and redeem ourselves."

"Redeems ourselves?" I asked, curious as to what she was alluding.

"Yes. For being whores!"

"I'm not a whore."

She chuckled profusely as she stood up and put her jacket on. "Marc, your sister and I remain close friends. She tells me everything."

"She's also a pathological liar," I said, downing my shot of espresso the moment it was presented, an act Amelia replicated.

"I know. That's why I only believe half the things she tells me, which nonetheless make you a very naughty lad."

After dropping a wad of cash on the table to cover the tab for the drinks, Amelia and I headed for the elevators.

"Your room or mine?" she asked.

"I have one of those bathtubs with water jets in it," I replied.

"Mine has a view of the bay and a bottle of Cristal in the fridge."

"Your room it is then!" I decided.

In the elevator I asked, "What exactly are you doing in town? You didn't come just to-"

"Absolutely not!" she flared, "I'm here for the expo."

"What expo?"

"The National Association of Women in the Media Convention and Trade Show expo. You know, NAWoMeCo!" She pronounced the ridiculous acronym with an effortless exactness and a smile.

"When we were together you always said how much you hated that group. Have you sold out?"

"No! I'm not going to it, I'm protesting it! If they're stupid enough to hold a rally of conservatism in a hotbed of liberalism then damn it, I'll be using my first amendment right, or, in the very least, the last shred of it that remains in these fascist United States."

Within ninety seconds of exiting the elevator we were in her room and on the bed fucking more violently than all the tawdry filthiness aggregated in our marriage, quickly dissolving any notion that I was a gentle lover. Sex is so much better when you're with a fellow whore, especially if she's your ex-wife and you still love her.

DEPARTURES

"Cristal and cunnilingus in San Francisco!" Amelia narrated as we greeted the unexpected sunrise. We'd both been misled in to believing it had been mere moments since we'd got to the room and began our latest affair. "Could life be any richer? I have my favorite Frenchman, Louis Roederer, in my mouth and this handsome stranger between my legs!"

"Why don't you put your favorite American in your mouth?" I suggested.

"That's disgusting!" Amelia chastised, her voice still slurred with inebriation.

"What?" I balked. I'd been in her mouth countless times throughout the night, making her sudden refusal absurd.

"My favorite American is Oprah."

"I meant me."

"You think just because I'm willing to have sex with you for seven consecutive hours you're suddenly my favorite American?"

"Ok, favorite Washingtonian."

"That sounds reasonable. But why do you care what I think of you? You don't want to get married again do you?" she teased.

"Absolutely not. Marriage is so archaic... so last century... an institution for codependents. Put simply, marriage is for morons."

"That's the most intelligent thing I've ever heard you say. I should write that down."

On cue the telephone rang, as it always does in civilized times when it senses humans to be delving in to topics too trecherous to explore without harm.

Amelia answered the phone with anticipation followed by a stream of joyous exclamations. "My flight was very nice... no, they flew me first class... that's fantastic dear, you'll have to email the photos... no, not bored at all. I'm starting to believe everything you told me about San Francisco to be a lie... oh, well

I'll talk to you later. I love you too, bye." She hung up the phone and rolled back over on top of me.

"Who was that?" I asked.

"My fiancé," she replied deviously. "He's in Beijing for some conference of international, uh… people. You know? Those politician people…"

"Ambassadors?" I posed.

"Yes!" she lit up.

"Didn't you just agree that marriage was last century?" I asked.

"Yes. But this is not a conventional marriage," she said as she got out of bed and walked across the room nude to fetch her robe. She didn't mind that the curtains had been opened and everyone in the city with a view of the hotel could probably see her naked ass and all its marvelousness. "He's the son of a powerful New England senator who was the son of a senator just as his father was before him. Blah-blah-blah. It's his job to produce an heir to the Massachusetts throne in Congress. Unfortunately he's the biggest homo you'd ever meet. But, unlike most homos, he's very dedicated to the traditions of his family. So we've worked out a compromise."

"What do you get out of it?"

"A giant summer house on Martha's Vineyard which he says I can inhabit all-year-round when the campaign is over, so while he's in DC with his man Troy, I'll be in Edgartown with god knows who. I get notoriety for being the wife of someone who's likely to ascend to the rank of Senator, or maybe Governor. He has the looks for it. I'll show you a picture! And, if I'm clever enough, I'll get children."

"Something your last husband wouldn't give you," I pointed.

"Yeah, the bastard." She took her wallet from her handbag and showed me the collection of pictures she had of her trophy husband. As an occasional bisexual, I can say with confidence he was fairly good looking, very WASPy, definitely from New England. He looked like an Abercrombie & Fitch model all grown up and ready to chair a sub-committee.

"Marc, do you still smoke those cigarettes?" she asked.

"Yes. Why?"

"I'd like one," she fluttered her eyes, an attempt to make me feel sorry for her, which I didn't.

"One last puff before you're a rural mother-to-be?"

"Yes. A frumpy, miserable, housewife married to a queer. I have so much to look forward to! If I'm lucky he'll get outed in a sex scandal and I'll land a million dollar advance for a book deal. I'll write a tell-all on what it was like being deceived." She cackled wildly after this statement. "I'll get started on the manuscript when we fly to St. Bart's for our honeymoon. Surely I'll have plenty of time on my hands."

From my coat, which lay crumpled on the floor next to the bed, I took two cigarettes, lit them both, and handed her one. She puffed on it a couple times, foolishly, like it was her first even though it wasn't, and started laughing as she stood by the open window, the light turning her elegant robe translucent, concealing nothing. Her breasts looked amazing in the light and I think she did this because the robe was tied just so above her waist it gave them a bit of a flattering lift, not that they were saggy.

"I can't believe this!" Amelia dallied, "We've slept together again. I love it. You're so cool to let me do this."

"Do what?"

"Use you like a piece of meat."

"I'm not the only piece of meat here honey."

"Don't be so coy. And don't *honey* me... When I leave you in an hour you'll be crushed. Admit it, *honey!*"

"As fascinating as you are Amelia, when you leave, preferably before I wake up from the nap I plan to take, it will be a relief. You know that."

"Yes. But pretend you'll be crushed," she teased. "Tell me you need me and that I broke your fucking heart when I left you." As she said this she slipped her hand through the front of my robe and petted by erection.

"You left me? I thought I left you." I stood up, closed my robe, and extinguished my cigarette.

"You're probably right. But in my book... the one I'm writing about my marriage to you, I leave you on the Pont de Neuf after discovering you're a sociopath." She giggled a bit, "And a bisexual."

"What trash you write. It's probably going to sell as well as that piece of compost my sister wrote."

I went in to the bathroom and started a shower. When I came out to get dressed I found Amelia had gone to my hotel room to shower as well. Had I been told I was meeting with my ex-wife before coming to the hotel I would have avoided the encounter with any rational measure possible. Never would I have expected Amelia to be so changed, so free and gloriously aloof. In a way, as she'd predicted and desired, I would be crushed when she fled San Francisco without me.

In my hotel room we gave ourselves a final primp in the mirror when there was a persistent knock on the suite's door. When I answered it I found young Giuseppe standing there in tears. He was not crying out of grief but rage.

"There you are!" he burst upon seeing me.

"What's wrong?" I asked.

"Everything. I need your help. I've had a horrible night. Halston and I had a fight and he left saying he was going for a walk to cool down but when I woke up this morning he was still gone."

I knew immediately Halston had not gone for a walk to ease his temperament. Rather, he'd abandoned Giuseppe as he'd done all his muses – cruelly and in the midst of bitterness.

Amelia came out of the bathroom fully dressed and rolling her suitcase behind her just like a flight attendant on her way to work.

"Hello," she said to Giuseppe. "Are you an escort?"

"Amelia!" I cursed, "This is Giuseppe, Halston's-"

"I am Halston's nothing!" he asserted madly. "I don't even know that man anymore."

"What are you doing in America?" Amelia asked him.

"I'm an artist."

"An artist? You smell too good to be an artist," she seduced him. Giuseppe very much liked Amelia's demeanor of flattery and flagrance. She alone provided the tumultuous moment an air of calm and elegance.

"I'm Italian," he said as needlessly as an alien explaining they hailed from Mars.

"I know. I'm not blind and deaf." Amelia kissed me on the cheek and added, "Gentlemen it's been fun but I'm off to Beijing."

"What? You didn't say you were leaving San Francisco today," I said.

"Ah-hah! You're devastated Marc!"

"More than devastated. Suicidal." I suddenly reminded myself of William Zofield and how I'd completely forgot to tell Amelia of his death.

We followed Amelia to the elevator and down to the lobby where she checked out. Outside the stately hotel we waited for the concierge to fetch her a taxi.

"You know, I was in Seattle not two weeks ago. I should have called you," she admitted.

"What were you doing in Seattle?"

"My crazy brother! He's decided he's a painter now. He's living in one of those converted warehouses near the stadiums. I forget the name of the neighborhood. Does Seattle have a Soho like London and New York do?"

"It's called So*do*. South of Downtown."

"Oh. Anyway, he's become a painter. So cliché, but I visit him every now and then. It's probably just a mid-life crisis. Next time… maybe we could schedule a little rendezvous?"

"If you're lucky," I replied. We hugged as her cab arrived.

"Take care of yourself Marc," she said finally and got in the taxi.

"You do the same Amelia," I responded just before she shut the door. She then rolled down the window and said quietly so neither Giuseppe or even the cab driver could hear, "Happy birthday." With that said she was taken away down Mason Street.

"That was your ex-wife?" Giuseppe inquired.

"Yes. What a fool I am to let her go."

"You're not a fool."

Another cab pulled up in front of us with Katrin in it. She was dressed in the same clothes as the day before, carrying with her a frayed leather duffle bag and the suitcase of manuscripts William had left behind.

"Good morning," I greeted her. She did not return any acknowledgement of kindness. She had the grimmest look on her face and I correctly assumed she hadn't slept all night.

"This is yours," she said, handing me the suitcase filled with her father's ultimate works.

"I can't take these," I replied vehemently.

"You have to. He left a note inside the suitcase stating I was not to touch them. He said to give them to a real writer. One who knew what the power of prose was and respected it." She was noticeably stung by the letter.

"So? Why give them to me?"

"According to this note," she furthered, pulling out the handwritten letter from the duffle bag, "I am to leave the manuscripts with a Mr. Marc Mulberry and nobody else. Not even his brother, who he entrusted his entire estate to."

"His estate?" Giuseppe entreated, "He left you nothing?"

"He said he couldn't leave anything to me," she grumbled. "Something about British law and taxes and how much I'd be in debt seeing how I'm an American. But all that doesn't matter. He wants you to have his work Marc. His last wish was for you to take them to New York."

"But I refuse Katrin. I'm not going to New York. I insist you take them there with you, it's where you're headed anyway after all this. I can give you the name of my editor. He'll take good care of these and you." I gave her back the suitcase and she placidly accepted it. She said nothing more, not even goodbye, and got back in the cab. But as she drove off, in the same manner as Amelia before her, she purposely left on the curb something she shouldn't have: the suitcase.

"I can't believe her!" I growled as I quickly grabbed the case of writings just before an airport shuttle van would have surely run over them.

"What's the big deal?" Giuseppe prodded. "Just accept them. Any writer would kill to get to read those things. Maybe the publisher who picks them up will ask you to write a forward for one of them. It'll be an honor."

"I know that," I said. "But I don't need the honor. And it just doesn't interest me."

"Doesn't interest you?" His anger was suddenly refueled. "How can it not? The man is... *was* a legend. Sure, people may not realize it at this moment. But in a hundred years the 20th-Century's literature will be defined by only a dozen voices. One of those is going to be William Zofield's. You have in your hand there possibly his greatest work, unpublished and raw, in all its fiery glory and you say it doesn't interest you!"

"To tell you the truth," I explained, "William Zofield's work always seemed a bit drippy to me. Too ornamental and shallow. Stories that take place in too beautiful of times to believe. And so melodramatic they make a modern day soap opera appear Shakespearean."

"Shit! What time is it?" Giuseppe boomed. "I have to get to the ship. We leave at nine o'clock."

"I doubt he'd leave without you," I soothed, even though I knew that was exactly what Halston had done. In all likelihood Halston had left town last night and was sailing toward Santa Barbara with the hopes of picking up another "actor" on the same pier he'd plucked Giuseppe from.

The measure of a true luxury hotel is the amenities they provide to their guests which are nothing but disposable, extravagant, and superfluous. This was the case at the Fairmont as they provided to their suite inhabitants the unlimited daily use of a brand new BMW sport sedan to anyone who asked.

"It's only eight-fifty!" Giuseppe cried with optimism as we climbed in to the opulent car.

"What about your things?" I asked him.

"I don't care. I just want to get to the ship."

I drove away from the hotel as quickly as possible but was reminded of how cautious I should be on these foreign streets after nearly taking a wrong downhill turn on Washington Street. For some bizarre reason the person who laid out San Francisco designed all the streets to be pointed uphill, so when one finds himself at the top of the Nob he must really search for a way down. Luckily, Hyde Street itself obliged traffic of both directions despite it also accommodating cable cars, which no matter how in the wrong, always seemed to assume the right of way over pedestrians and other vehicles.

"What is this all about?" I asked Giuseppe as he nervously tapped his foot on the floor of the car.

"We had a fight. Just a little fight."

"That's obvious," I said. "What about?" His only response was a glare that said 'you don't want to know.'

We arrived at the pier to find nothing but a throng of tourists snapping pictures in front of the historic ships and feasting on carnival style fare you could find in any American town. The only thing missing from the scene was the New Florentine, now gone, surely in pursuit of the next gorgeous landscape.

Giuseppe did not need to leave the car and inspect the end of the pier to see if in fact he'd just barely missed the boat. We both knew then Halston, a coward when it came to mending a relationship, had exited town many hours earlier.

"This must have been more than just a little fight," I muttered as we began the drive back up the hill to the hotel.

"Yes. It was. It was the truth," Giuseppe divulged at last.

"What did you say?"

"Nothing at first. It was he who did all the talking. He got very drunk with your sister and Tom yesterday afternoon. When he came to get dressed for dinner I said something about how I loved all our new friends. He pointed out they were *his* friends and I should consider myself lucky to be in the presence of so many minds. I said I was. Then he asked why I wasn't trying to bed Bryan Madden, the movie producer."

"And why aren't you?" I countered.

"When you're born without money or privilege you sometimes have to do things you don't want to in order to get where you're going. Sometimes a person will say they're something other than what they are to fool those who believe they know one's true intentions. An aspiring dancer would not be let in to freely wander the halls of Julliard to converse with its students and instructors. But someone in disguise, a rogue might be."

"I don't follow. You're a dancer, not an actor?" I asked. So far good analogies had escaped Giuseppe.

"No Marc! I'm a writer. You told me that yourself. And now that I've come out of the closet with it I'm not going back in." His declaration quickly escalated in volume until he was nearly yelling. It was his most theatrical performance yet.

"What's so shameful about being a writer?" I asked. I'd always thought of writers as being a modern form of nobility.

"Nothing. But selling one's body in order to become one is."

"You sold yourself? How much did he pay you?" I asked, turning the car around.

"Nothing. That makes me the biggest whore of all. I did this all for free."

"But you're going to get published," I reminded him.

"You really think so?" he asked, completely unaware of the clout I held within the publishing sphere.

"I'm Marc Mulberry. If I tell my publisher to print your book they'll do it."

The hotel we returned to was not the same refuge of quiet dignity we'd left. Outside the lobby an inundation of vulgar, hungry media had gathered. They're purpose to further expose and catch a glimpse of a movie star who'd been secretly filmed from a nearby balcony with his gay lover, another Hollywood personality, doing what lovers do when alone in a hotel room in a city as amorous as San Francisco. Every cable news network was there, each of them already broadcasting the surveillance style tape of two men humping madly. It was the first time that such pop-culture scandal rubbish had been trumpeted as news. We were in the uneasy presence of history being made. It was both glamorous and sickening.

"I say we get to the airport as soon as possible," I suggested.

"The airport? Are you deporting me?" Giuseppe sneered.

"No. Why would I deport you? You're my friend. I'm assuming you have no place to live so I'll take you back to Whidbey Island with me. We'll work on finalizing that book of yours. You can even rummage through what Zofield left behind with me."

"I don't want you to get the wrong idea Marc. When I said people sometimes do things they normally wouldn't in order to get where they're going I meant that I was sleeping with Halston in order to meet his friends. But I'm not gay."

"Neither am I," I made sure, mildly upset he'd misinterpreted my offer of apprenticeship.

Just before arriving at San Francisco International Airport, Mr. Tavolo had but one final secret to reveal. "I'm not exactly in America legally." So instead of boarding a flight where our nationalities would be scrutinized, I opted to borrow the Fairmont's BMW for a quick 14-hour drive up the winding Pacific Coast Highway, stopping only once in a town known as Florence, Oregon with the sole intent of purchasing a postcard and to refuel. Back in Seattle we dropped the car off at the Olympic, the same hotel where four days prior I'd parked my waiting Alfa Romeo, a car Giuseppe nearly fainted with adoration over upon seeing. A car as pristinely maintained as mine was rare, he said, even in Italy.

WE, THE FORTUNATE

The annual summit of the council of miserable souls — a group I was a permanent member of - had officially concluded and I was free. I'd gained a protégé, something I'd later realize to be a subconscious and lucrative pursuit, and was now returning home to a vineyard of solace and quiet happiness. More ironic than it was coincidental, Giuseppe knew everything there was to viticulture and winemaking having worked as a teenager in the vineyards of Antinori in the town of Bolgehri not far from his native Antignano. Between our relentless two-person writing workshops we became partners in creation, of both wine and words, and nothing more, as I'm sure some corrupts minds have speculated.

America's greatest writers were never to reassemble on the New Florentine again for a number of reasons. The boat itself was seized when Halston reached Barcelona and was arrested for tax evasion and extradited to Louisiana where he spent some time in prison, not only for his failure to pay Uncle Sam and all the other governments he'd proclaimed to be a citizen of in his travels, but also overdue child support due to the his wife Zelda who he'd failed to divorce before abandoning her and their two children some 16 years prior. During his two years in prison, Halston Levy would pen his seminal work, *Gangbang*, the story of the exquisite pleasures some homosexual men find prison to be. In a letter addressed to me just a week after he was locked up, Halston wrote, "Marc, I'm in heaven! Every day is spent working out in the gym and all night we fuck like beasts. It's divine, I never want to leave. If I knew incarceration was going to be so hot I would have pleaded guilty the second they caught me." The publicity surrounding his arrest, trial, and imprisonment was a PR dream for Halston. When he left prison and *Gangbang* reached the number one spot on the *New York Times* bestsellers list, I couldn't help but suspect the whole thing to be a dazzling, but fabricated spectacle.

Bryan Madden and Olive Snow would remain married and miserable, even after Bryan's career in Hollywood was complicated by the scandal surrounding his encounter with the movie star. Together they'd fade in to obscurity on a ranch in Montana where they claimed to be raising horses and children. The only thing they raised was eyebrows for in a small, conservative town there are no secrets. The Madden-Snow residence was revered as the local freak house where immoral sex parties were held and sin seemed to be manufactured. Byran Madden's planned book, *The Glamour Factory*, never made it to bookshelves. I frequently wondered what happened to the manuscript and sometimes questioned if I should offer to help him finish the book. As absurd as his actions were on the New Florentine, I couldn't help but feel sympathy for a man who was burning in an undoubtedly painful hell of his own making.

Tom Reynolds kept on writing over-patriotic schlock about war and terrorism which continued to sell as well as always. Ashley remained in San Francisco until Tom left a week after they'd begun their affair when he realized he loved his wife more than anything. Living sparsely off her book royalties, Ashley decided both San Francisco and America were beneath her and she'd tried to reinvent herself in Venice, then Paris, and eventually Berlin, where she met a charming engineer who was rather bland, but she married regardless. Ashley Mulberry never published her memoir on her experience aboard the New Florentine, even though she took a $50,000 advance on the project, which she was forced to repay five years after the deadline. After a sudden divorce, and a year of sullen drunkenness, she joined Alcoholics Anonymous and became a licensed massage therapist, opening her own spa in Reinickendorf, a Berlin suburb renowned for its inexpensive prostitutes, airport noise, and a burgeoning human trafficking industry.

Katrin Zofield began to age visibly after the death of her father and was no longer considered the foremost authority on relationships in New York City. Without her looks and her wit out of vogue she moved to Los Angeles to start over but ended up dead in a car accident while returning from the beach via Topanga Canyon.

Amelia Haughton married her politician fiancé. The wedding was flawless, the children beautiful and timed perfectly three years apart. The only thing that kept Amelia from becoming first lady of Massachusetts was, when during the midst of her husband's gubernatorial election campaign, a male intern accused the candidate of groping him in an elevator. The candidate made a forceful denial of the accusations and was initially successful in deflecting scandal. Several weeks passed and the campaign appeared to be unfazed, and poll numbers indicated the candidate was still likely to win election. That was until surveillance video of the candidate doing a lot more than just groping the fragile intern appeared on the internet. The campaign inevitably failed, the politician was without a job, and Amelia grew bored of playing the role of arm candy to a failed politician. She wound up back at my vineyard the same weekend she broke it off with her husband. Together we established an arrangement of our own. She would be my occasional wife and I her dignified rebound. We didn't renew our vows but remained close friends.

William Zofield's lost work was better left unread. After returning home and reviewing his final passages of fiction I found him to have been a crazy old man, just as everyone had warned. His stories made no sense. Characters were angry without reason and spoke like children, not the adults they were purported to be. The characters often had random and casual sex with each other and many of them ended up killing themselves after experiencing trivial humiliation or a highly gratifying illumination. After much contemplation I decided the manuscripts would remain unpublished, not wanting to taint the body of work Zofield had managed to yield long ago while young and sober.

Giuseppe Tavolo would become a great writer and live in Chateau Mulberry until he could afford his own vineyard, one he'd cultivate not one mile from my own. I would witness Giuseppe wed the first authentic Italian woman who stumbled upon our village. Together they'd produce a family of six children and I would become to their children Uncle Marc, the mysterious goofy loner whose part-time girlfriend was always out of town and who for some reason was a better friend to their father than anyone. The octet and I would travel together, most often through Italy and specifically to Florence in the winters where we bought a villa in the Oltrarno just off the Via Romano. The modest stone house had a view of the Giardino di Boboli and made the perfect pied-a-terre to escape to whenever the weather of Puget Sound became too dreary to tolerate.

As for Marc Mulberry, I became a writer again. With an acquired family and a companion in creation as unlikely as Giuseppe Tavolo, the solace sought by remaining true to the land and respecting self-sufficiency finally bore harvest. Together we were philosophers, our most active pursuit to examine the worth society placed on artists, most specifically the writer. We came to understand that the public at large either loved or loathed those who wrote words, thought up things that never happened and created people who never existed. Some people revile a person who is not a member of the working class and who does not produce goods or services of a set worth. And then there are those who desire to be us, to work without a schedule or a supervisor, knowing that it is not products emerging from an assembly line that live forever but ideas and stories that stand the test of time. If they're any good.

The born artist knows they are unlike the majority of society. They know that what they work on is unnecessary for survival, yet without the enlightenment their contribution affords, survival becomes unappealing. An intrepid writer, someone who dabbles in the medium of communication as their art form, will find they are dealt the most confounding paradox. Their work is liquid and internalized more than any other art. It is consumed by the masses and manipulated in to other forms of media. It motivates and matures within those who let it. Nonetheless, the written word, as harmless as it may seem for it just sits there and does nothing, can either destroy or nurture those who dare tamper with it.

Acknowledgements

Mom and Dad, you're the best!

Ian, thank you for putting up with all my bullshit.

Kristeen, thank you so much for all the help you've given me on this book. Your honest feedback has been invaluable.

Coming Soon

Marc Mulberry will return in…

Murder At Mulberry Manor

The second book in the Marc Mulberry Series.